Praise for Kitty and Rebecca:

'I read it to my sons and
we laughed ourselves inside out.'
Ed Byrne

'Mesmerizing and funny, and
reminded me of Lemony Snicket.'
Ama, age 7, *Toppsta*

'Children may find their bedside table raided by
parents eager to get aboard the laugh-train!'
Jesse Armstrong (writer of *Peep Show,*
***Succession, Four Lions*)**

'An absolutely thrilling adventure!'
Spirited, age 7, *Toppsta*

'Captivating illustrations.
Children ... are likely to be enthralled.'
Children's Books Ireland

'The most magical adventure stories.
I am so looking forward to the next book to
find out what happens.'
Kenzah, age 8

HARRY HEAPE is an artist, a visionary and a very successful none-of-your-businessman. A shy and quiet man, Harry lives and writes on the edge of a magical forest where he spends any spare time that he has collecting enamel badges.

REBECCA BAGLEY lives in Bath (the city, not A BATH, although she did have one once) where she draws pictures so she doesn't have to get a real job. When she's not hanging out in the world of children's books, she'll probably be in a headstand, plotting how best to smuggle a husky into her flat without anyone noticing.

Indiana
BONeS
and the Invisible City

Illustrated by
HARRY HEAPE   **REBECCA BAGLEY**

faber

First published in the UK in 2023
First published in the US in 2023
by Faber and Faber Limited
The Bindery,
51 Hatton Garden,
London, EC1N 8HN
faber.co.uk

Typeset in Amaranth by M Rules
This font has been specially chosen to support reading

Printed and bound by
CPI Group (UK) Ltd, Croydon CR0 4YY

A CIP record for this book
is available from the British Library

ISBN 978–0–571–35354–5

Printed and bound in the UK on FSC paper in line with our continuing
commitment to ethical business practices, sustainability and the environment.
For further information see faber.co.uk/environmental-policy

1 3 5 7 9 10 8 6 4 2

It may be a little funusual, but I would like to dedicate this book to a bus and to a boy.

The bus is a large yellow American school bus that travels around Bradford, spreading the joy of reading. It is part of the wonderful work of the National Literacy Trust. I've had some of my favourite times as a writer on board this magical bus. Thank you Imran, Dale and Nabeelah.

The boy is my friend Eddie.

Love to the boy. Love to the bus.

xx HH xx

Prologue

Waaaaaah! Hello again from Sir Harold of Heape!

Welcome back to each and every last one of you, my much-beloved story crunchers. I'm super-excited and positively giddy with gladness to be back. I am as itchy as a tiny toe in a sandy sock to get started, but we

must-must-must have a mini recap (the size of a flea's kneecap) so we all know fizzactly where we are up to.

Here are the most slimportant pieces of funformation that you need before we dive-bomb into Chapter One.

- Our heroes are Indiana Bones and Aisha Ghatak. Indiana is a magical talking dog from another dimension. He likes sandwiches, sleeping and having his belly tickled. Aisha is a kick-ass archaeologist who is

Brave + Clever + Kind = Awesome.

- The Lonely Avenger is a two-thousand-year-old knight who left an extraordinary amount of treasure hidden somewhere on Planet Earth. Aisha and Indiana have been mega close to finding it – TWICE.

- At the end of *Indiana Bones and the Lost Library*, they met the knight and his dog, Amie – who turned out to be Indiana Bones's real-life mum! The Avenger had used ancient magic to preserve himself in a chamber under a ruined library in Ephesus, in Turkey, and he told Indiana and Aisha he'd hidden the treasure in *the best place in the world*.

- Before the knight and Amie crumbled to dust because the spell had been broken, the Avenger gave Aisha a key, which

was crucial to finding the treasure, as well as a load of magic potions and an invisibility shield.

- Bad guys are also after the treasure (boo): slippery Sir Henry Lupton (known as the Serpent), who has been looking for the treasure all his life; the equally greedy Philip Castle, who thinks he is the rightful heir; and a hapless, smelly fool called Ringo.

Bad guys come with bad news, and the baddest news is that they ambushed Aisha and took the key . . .

Boom. Boom. Boom.

Let's go.

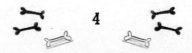

1

Fee-Fi-Fo-Fum

On a dark London evening, two shady figures stood high on a hotel balcony, eye-spying on the office of Sir Henry Lupton in the building opposite, known as the Gherkin. They had just watched his evil sidekick Philip Castle go out for food and were ready to make a move.

5

Aisha Ghatak and Celia pulled on balaclavas to hide their faces.

'When I tell you, jump on my back,' said Celia. 'We are going to zipwire across, break in and steal back your key. We have less than ten minutes before Castle returns with a belly full of pizza.'

Aisha watched with admiration, and a little shiver, as Celia fired one end of the zipwire across the expanse of space, where it stuck firmly to the exterior of the Gherkin. She then threaded the other end of the zipwire through the handles of a room-service trolley and secured it to the hotel balcony, pulling it super-taut and tight. Her dad's new partner had turned out to be a rather skilled cat

burglar rather than an insurance officer. She maintained that she was a loss adjuster of sorts: she helped people adjust their losses by stealing back things that had been stolen from them – jewellery, mostly.

'Seriously?' asked Aisha. 'We are actually going to do this?'

'We are,' answered Celia. 'One small thing – maybe don't mention *every* aspect of this evening to your dear father. Deal?'

'Deals on wheels,' Aisha replied with a grin.

'LET'S GO!' said Celia.

Aisha clamped herself onto Celia's back, and the cat burglar leaped into the night. Grabbing the handles of the little silver trolley, they flew through the air faster than fox fart through

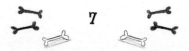

a farmyard, landing with a soft *badumpsh* against the Gherkin.

Swiftly and silently, they abseiled down the glassy exterior of the sleek building until they were outside Lupton's office. Smoother than a mole in a velvet tuxedo, Celia pulled out her glass-cutting equipment and sliced a small circle in the window. Then she reached inside, unlocked it, and they were in.

Just a metre away, Ringo slumbered on a large leather sofa. Aisha noticed his trademark rings glinting on his enormous naughty fingers. Snoring loudly, he shifted from one big chubby buttock to the other and broke wind. Half waking, he sat up, stretched, and opened his eyes.

Aisha darted over and pulled a little bottle labelled **Sopor** out of her pocket. It was one of the knight's potions. She pulled out its cork stopper and wafted it gently under Ringo's bulbous beak. The big man's eyes began to close again. He mumbled something about a pigeon and loving his mummy, then fell back asleep, sucking his thumb.

Our hero couldn't help but smile down at him as she breathed a sigh of relief. Turning round, her mouth popped open with amazeclonk. In the time it had taken Aisha to waft a potion under Ringo's hooter, Celia had located Lupton's safe. It was behind a large portrait of the Serpent on the wall next to his desk.

'Egomaniac baddies are so predictable,' she said with a grin, twisting the safe's dial.

A few clicks later and the heavy door swung open.

'Easier than blowing a raspberry on a baby's belly,' said Celia, pulling out the jewel-encrusted key they'd come for. She looked at her watch. 'Two minutes. Not bad. Time to skedaddle.'

Before they could move, a loud voice thundered through the room: 'Fee-fi-fo-fum, I smell the blood of a burglar man. Is that you, Ghatak?'

Aisha knew immediately that the voice belonged to the Serpent. Sir Henry Lupton had obviously mistaken Celia for Aisha's father.

They slowly turned round ... but, weird as a beard, the office was empty. On the far wall a large TV screen blinked to life and on it, the size of a dustbin lid, was the unmistakable face of the Serpent, incandescent with rage.

'Intruders!' he shouted, like a demented dalek. 'How dare you! I shall have you thrown in jail!'

Aisha and Celia stared at the screen, rooted to the spot, as Lupton pulled out a mobile phone.

'Castle, you nincompoop, where the blazes are you? The Ghataks are in the office and you are NOT!' He tapped at a keyboard furiously, then yelled down the phone. 'My on-street surveillance shows you are HAVING A PIZZA! Get back right now and apprehend them. Fail

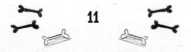

me and you will be fired! Finished for ever! The Grandmas will see to that!'

Lupton leaned into the camera, making his angry face even bigger on the screen, and whispered viciously, 'Listen, filthy Ghataks, I have bad news for you – I know *exactly* where to look for the treasure. In a matter of days, it will be mine, along with something else even more delicious.'

Aisha, frightened and angry, couldn't listen to the snake for another moment and switched off the TV.

'Let's go,' said Celia. They sprinted from Lupton's office into a long, wide corridor. At the end of the hallway, the lift was on its way up to their floor. Disaster, dear readers, as they

realised that this was their only exit and Castle would soon be upon them.

Suddenly Aisha remembered the invisibility shield the Avenger had given her, which she now carried everywhere. Quick as a frog in a Ferrari, she pulled it off her back. On the reverse of the shield were three precious gemstones: an emerald with the word **Visibilis** underneath, a ruby above the word **Invisibilis**, and a sapphire, like the ones that she, her father and Indiana wore. Under this was written **Invisibilia Videre**. Aisha had not yet had time to explore what all this meant, but she was about to find out. Gulping, she pressed the ruby with her thumb. She hoped this would turn the shield invisible – and it did!

'Crouch!' she whispered urgently to Celia.

They squatted down behind the invisible barrier just as the lift doors opened. Castle burst out, running along the corridor. He passed right by our hidden heroes and into Lupton's office.

Aisha and Celia dashed for the lift and rode down to the ground floor. As they exited the Gherkin, a sporty green car screeched to a halt at the kerb and honked its horn. Grinning at them from behind the wheel was our book's hairy hero and Aisha's favourite ladoo, Mr Indiana Bones.

'That went rather well, I thought!' said Celia, holding up the key in triumph as they sped away back to their friend Julimus's apartment.

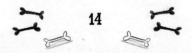

'You got it!' Indiana beamed.

But for Aisha it did not feel like a victory at all. It was true they had the precious key back, but they DIDN'T know where the treasure was. Lupton did, and would have it in a few days. This was terribubble news.

In fact, my lovely book munchers, to Aisha it was worse than that. It felt like a catastrophe, wrapped up inside a bad banana, on a broken barbecue. What on earth were they going to do now?

2

The Good Team Assemble

The next morning at Julimus's, Dr Satnam Ghatak gathered the friends together for a meeting, to decide what to do next. Aisha was still very glum from the previous evening's bad news and was impatient to get on with things.

'Right!' said Dr Ghatak, addressing everybody with great intent. 'We need a battle plan. The clock is ticking. It is time for us to mobilise.'

'What are you thinking, Dad?' Aisha asked, looking brighter.

'Well, what started with you and me as a hunt for treasure has now escalated,' said Dr Ghatak. 'Lupton has revealed his hand and we need to up our game. Instead of working individually, we must gather a marvellous, intelligent team.'

'Yes!' Aisha agreed. 'Obviously Julimus and Jovis for starters.'

'A wonderful addition to any team,' said Satnam. Julimus smiled, wearing a shabby suit as usual, and his son, Jovis, gave a couple of funny little bows.

'Who else?' said Aisha.

'How about Edith?' Indiana Bones suggested, thinking of their old friend and lodger at home back in Oxford.

'Perfect,' agreed Satnam. 'She's one of the smartest people I know. Anyone else?'

'Mr Charman and Mr Dukes,' said Aisha. 'They have so much knowledge of the world and they can help with any kind of travel arrangements we might need.'

'Very good,' said Dr Ghatak, writing the names down on a list. 'Who else?'

Aisha thought for a second. 'Dimitar!' she said. Dimitar Vakondember was a man she and Indiana had met on the train to Istanbul. An inventor who worked for the Bureau of Missing International Artefacts in Hungary. 'He's very knowledgeable and he hates the Serpent.'

'Yay!' said Indiana. 'I'm glad you suggested him. He has the best toys. Remember Old Meg, Mr Vakondember's flying machine?'

'Of course,' said Aisha. 'She looked like a cross between a bird, a boat and a bat.'

'Okay then, Dimitar too,' said Satnam. 'Old Meg does sound fun,' he added with a twinkle in his eye. 'We must contact them all and then we will travel in Julimus's camper van to Oxford, where we will put together an action plan.'

Indiana Bones wagged his tail a little and settled down while the others bustled about making calls. He liked the thought of going home to Oxford, but he was fed up too. Last night he'd dreamed about being with his mum, Amie, in Skara Brae, and right now he was finding it hard to care about Lupton and the treasure. The sapphire in his collar was glowing and pulsing ever so gently. This precious stone had come from his home in Skara Brae, on the Orkney Islands in the far north of Scotland, and it connected him to the spirit world. Indiana did not understand why his sapphire was awake; he only knew that it was.

From his position on the floor, he glanced up at the jar on the mantelpiece, which held

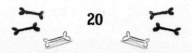

the sandy remains of Amie and the Lonely Avenger that Aisha had rescued from the magical room under the library in Ephesus.

Hearing a big sigh, Julimus looked at Indiana and thought he understood.

'Maybe you could scatter your mum's ashes somewhere special,' he suggested, bending down and giving the dog's ears a loving rub. 'It might help.'

Indiana looked up at gentle Julimus and gave his friend the softest of woofs.

Later that afternoon our friends arrived, all together, outside Charman and Dukes, an old glass-fronted travel agency in the centre of Oxford. They were welcomed by Mr Charman,

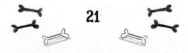

21

who immediately turned the shop's 'Open' sign to 'Closed' and pulled down the blind to cover the glass door.

On the journey from London, the Good Team had agreed that it was time to share Indiana's secret with Mr Charman and Mr Dukes: that he was a magical dog who could talk. Mr Charman and Mr Dukes were, of course, surprised, but they promised to keep it to themselves.

'We won't tell a soul,' they assured Dr Ghatak.

'We both know there is a great deal of magic in the world that is hidden from us mere mortals,' added wise old Mr Dukes. 'And, besides, we have a secret of our own too.'

Mr Charman and Mr Dukes led the team into the room at the back of the shop.

'It's been a while since we used *this* room,' said Mr Charman.

'Very true,' Mr Dukes said, nodding. 'Although there was a time just after the Second World War when we spent days and days down here, eating, sleeping and working.'

Mr Charman walked over to the bookcase on the far wall and pushed the spine of an old book with his index finger, as if he was ringing a doorbell. To the Good Team's amazement, the whole bookcase slid silently to the left, revealing a green leather door. They gasped and the hairs on the back of Aisha's neck prickled. Mr Charman unlocked the door and switched on a light, revealing a flight of stone steps.

The elderly travel agent led them down the hidden stairway to a basement room that was laid out a bit like an old-fashioned classroom. There was a horseshoe of desks and wooden chairs around the outer edge, with a large desk at the front, on which was a big radio and a pair of headphones. On the wall behind that desk was a yellowing map of Europe, curling at the corners, and a blackboard. There was a bulky television on a stand, and on another wall was an ancient telephone, with a handle to wind it up. At the back of the room was a smaller red door.

'During the war, Mr Charman and I worked for the British government,' explained Mr Dukes. 'With a friend, we met in this secret

room to brief the Prime Minister and the President of the United States of America, to help them with matters of national security.'

Aisha and Indiana were thrilled.

'That is *so* cool,' said Aisha, and she gave Mr Charman a big hug, which made him laugh and blush, then hug her back, like an awkward robot.

They all agreed it would be the perfect base for the Good Team.

Satnam, Celia and Julimus began to bring the HQ into the twenty-first century, dusting down the desks and plugging in laptops, screens and projectors they'd brought with them. Jovis printed out a large picture of Sir Henry Lupton to pin on the

wall. It was an important reminder that the Serpent must not be forgotten, not even for a moment.

Jovis disappeared upstairs to make a huge tray of tea for everyone, returning a few minutes later with the Ghataks' lodger and old friend, Edith Ellinor.

'Lovely to see you again, Edith,' said Mr Charman.

'It's a while since we were all down here,' said Mr Dukes, his eyes twinkling, and Aisha realised that Edith must be the friend he had mentioned earlier.

Julimus looked up from the laptop he'd been working on and said, 'Dimitar's here.' Aisha looked over to see Dimitar Vakondember's face

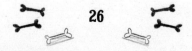

on the screen, smiling, from a thousand miles away in Budapest.

Satnam cleared his throat and addressed the room: 'Thank you all for coming. Aisha and Indiana have been hunting for the Avenger's treasure – an adventure that has taken them around the world. Hot on their heels has always been Sir Henry Lupton, who many of you know.'

'Hold on,' Aisha interrupted. 'So, who else knows Lupton?'

'I think we all do,' replied Edith. 'Mr Charman, Mr Dukes and I knew his father, Lord Horatio Lupton. We suspected him of mass looting throughout Europe during the war, and Mr Dukes worked undercover in his house in Casablanca.'

Dimitar joined in from the screen. 'I know the Serpent only too well. We at the Bureau of Missing International Artefacts have been chasing him for years. He has a habit of making others do his dirty work, so it has been impossible to trap him.'

Celia nodded. 'That has been my experience too.'

'It's time to coordinate our efforts,' said Satnam. 'Last night, the Serpent told Aisha and Celia that he knows exactly where the treasure is. If we are to have any chance of finding it first, we need to orchestrate his defeat.'

'He mentioned something else,' Aisha added. 'Something he described as *delicious*.'

'Friends, we have no idea what this is,' said

Satnam. 'But I think you'll agree, it does not sound good.'

'Did he say anything else, Aisha?' asked Edith.

'He threatened to sack Philip Castle if he didn't find us, and that the Grandmas – whoever they are – would see to finishing him,' Aisha replied.

'I've never heard of the Grandmas,' said Mr Charman.

'Nor I,' said Mr Dukes. 'Has anyone?'

The team all shook their heads.

'We need someone in charge here at our HQ,' Satnam announced. 'Someone to sit at this desk and organise our operations.' He looked around the room.

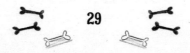

'There is only one person who could ever sit in that chair,' said Mr Dukes. 'The person who sat in it fifty years ago and briefed not only Mr Charman and myself but also several world leaders.'

'Who?' asked Indiana.

'Me,' said Edith Ellinor. She rolled up her sleeves, hitched up her tights and plonked a large bag on the floor beside the large desk. 'It feels wonderful to be back.'

Satnam and Aisha beamed at Edith. They could not imagine anyone better suited to lead the Good Team.

'Right!' said their sparky commander. 'How marvellous to be joined by so many friends, old and new! Alone, I don't think that any of us

could find the treasure. After all, it has been extremely well hidden for two thousand years. But together, I believe, we will be able to do these two wonderful things . . .'

She turned to the blackboard and wrote:

FIND TREASURE

FINISH LUPTON

'This is our mission. The Serpent is a beast who should be behind bars.'

Everyone nodded in agreement. Then they all sat at the desks and started sharing everything they knew about Sir Henry Lupton.

'I think the Serpent's weak points are the

people around him,' said Edith eventually. 'That is the way we will trap him.'

At last, it was time to take a break. They said their goodbyes to Dimitar, who told them he would head to England immediately so he could be properly part of the team that would try to bring down Lupton.

Heading upstairs, they became aware of a persistent banging on the shop door.

'I'm coming,' called Mr Dukes, rushing through the shop. He opened the front door and in slunk Philip Castle, with a baseball cap pulled low. Everyone stared.

Philip Castle put his fingers to his lips, grabbed a nearby chair and climbed onto it to

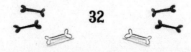

reach into the lampshade of the overhead light. He pulled out a small black electronic device, which agents of the Serpent had clearly been using to bug Charman and Dukes. Climbing down, he put the bug on the floor and crunched it under his shoe.

Mr Charman and Mr Dukes looked at each other, shocked at this revelation. But what they heard next was even more eye-popping.

'I've come to join you,' said Castle, his voice shaking. 'I'm sick of Lupton's rages. He's fired me and threatened to set the Grandmas on me – and, not to put too fine a point on it, I'm terrified.'

Nobody said a word, but they were all thinking the same thing. What was Castle

really up to? And who or what on earth were the Grandmas?

'I know Lupton's ways and his methods,' he continued. He reached into his pocket and pulled out a key. 'Here – this is a copy of the Avenger's key you took from Lupton's safe. It's the only one, I promise. It's an exact replica; even the jewels are real. I'm giving it to you. You have to believe me. I want to be on your side now.'

Indiana took a step forward and sniffed suspiciously at Castle. He smelled of unhappy potatoes, lies and bad meat. Indiana knew, without doubt, that they could not trust him. He showed this to his friends by barking loudly three times at Castle and then lying down flat, so that he resembled a hairy crocodile.

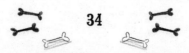

And yet ... hadn't Edith just said that the Serpent's weak points were those around him? In that moment, my friends, the balance of power seemed to shift back to the Good Team.

3

Gentlemen

'Why should we trust you?' the shabby-suited Julimus asked Castle. 'Perhaps you are a nasty little mole sent by Lupton to infiltrate us and steal our knowledge.'

Castle sneered. 'Sir Henry's lost interest in

you,' he said. 'He knows where the treasure is and that's all he cares about.'

Aisha's eyes narrowed and everyone stared at Castle. They knew he was right.

'You can think about it,' said Castle. 'And to prove you can trust me, I will give you another present.'

'What do you mean?' Satnam asked.

'A little information,' replied Castle. 'Every Wednesday, Lupton has lunch at his gentlemen's club in London. It's called Opulentos. He always eats in the Reading Room, which is the club's most exclusive dining area. He's there from midday until four. Maybe you could follow him for a change.'

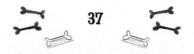

The Good Team exchanged looks. It was hard to trust one of Lupton's goons, but this did really seem like a gift.

Castle laughed nastily at their silence. 'Take your time. Think about how you want to use me. I am sure I can be very useful.' He started for the door, then turned and asked, 'Can I visit your bathroom before I go?'

Mr Dukes pointed him in the right direction, through the back office.

While Castle waddled off for a widdle, the Good Team huddled together.

'Can we trust him?' whispered Mr Dukes.

'No!' said Aisha. 'He's a worm and his boss is a snake.'

Indiana, still flat on the floor, growled in agreement.

'I say we trust the instincts of Indiana,' whispered Edith. 'We will politely decline.'

The rest of the gang nodded.

In the office and out of sight, Castle was on the hunt for something. 'Bingo,' he said, spotting the spare shop key hanging on a hook.

Quickly as a schmickley pickley he pulled out a huge blob of Blu-Tack from his jacket pocket. Lifting the spare key off the hook, he pressed a perfect copy of its shape into the putty. 'Trusting twerps,' he whispered to himself, replacing the key where he'd found it. Then he walked back into the shop.

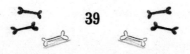

Aisha spoke up at once. 'It's a no from us, Mr Castle. Thank you for your offer, but we don't want you on our team.'

Castle smiled a fake smile, not really surprised. He had got what he came for and didn't mind hearing this news. 'Your loss, love,' he said, shrugging before slipping out of the front door without a backwards glance.

'He strikes me as a grade-A toad,' said Edith. 'We don't want him anywhere near us or our headquarters. Now, what do we think about Lupton's lunch?'

'Could be a trap,' said Mr Dukes.

'Could be an opportunity,' said Celia. 'And tomorrow is Wednesday. I, for one, think we should strike.'

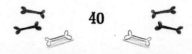

'Let's do it!' agreed Aisha. 'Indiana and I can get a disguise and follow him to the treasure.'

'But we need to try to get ahead, not just follow him,' said Celia.

Edith narrowed her eyes and thought hard. 'True. We must know precisely what the slippery rogue's plans are.'

'Do to him what he did to us! We should bug him!' said Mr Charman, still furious.

'That snake had the audacity to place a listening device in *our* shop,' added Mr Dukes, also fuming. 'Bug him back twice as hard, I say!'

'But who will bell the cat?' Edith said.

Since Castle left, Indiana had cheered up enormously and was now playing a

tremendous game of Tickle Monster under a table with Jovis. The small boy was laughing like a drain as Indiana stared hard at his armpits but never quite tickled them. At Edith's words, though, our scruffy pooch popped his head out.

'Excuse me?' he asked. 'Did someone say cats?'

'It's from a story, my dear,' Edith told him. 'A group of mice were discussing how to prevent a cat from eating them. One suggested that if a bell were hung around the cat's neck, they would hear it coming. The question was, which mouse would perform the dangerous task of putting a bell around the cat's neck? And what I am asking is, who will bug Lupton?'

'We will,' said Aisha without hesitation. 'Like I said, you can disguise me, and Indiana can be under my invisibility shield.' As she said this, she remembered that she still had to work out exactly what the shield's three settings could do: **Visibilis**, **Invisibilis** and **Invisibilia Videre**. 'I could pretend to be a young waiter.'

'Too dangerous,' said Dr Ghatak.

'I don't see anyone else here who could be disguised as a young waiter,' said a determined Aisha.

'Fair point,' her father admitted. 'In that case, we need a small bug and a quick, clever and, above all, safe plan.'

'I have a handbag full of bugs,' said Celia coolly.

'Excellent,' said Edith. 'Aisha will be in public, so the risk is minimal. While we work out how to make everything super-safe – Mr Charman, Mr Dukes, can I set you a special task?'

'Of course,' replied the elderly gentlemen of travel. 'We would be delighted.'

'I want you to find out all you can about the Grandmas,' instructed Edith. 'Whoever they are, they seem to have Castle spooked.'

'Right away,' said Mr Charman. 'And I know exactly where to start. An old friend of ours worked on the crime desk at the *Sunday Times* for years. We will arrange to meet him for tea and pick his brains!'

And with that he and Mr Dukes headed purposefully out of the door.

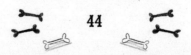

Edith turned to the others. 'Julimus, can you sort out a waiter's uniform for Aisha? It will need to match the ones they have at Opulentos. Satnam and Celia, I think you should continue trying to work out the location of the treasure. If the bugging fails, we will need a plan B. Lastly, I'll start making a list of things Dimitar may be able to assist with when he arrives.'

The team worked long into the evening on their various assignments. Jovis brought tea and snacks at regular intervals, and played Fifty-Five Favourite Sandwiches with Indiana.

Satnam and Celia returned to their research on the Avenger's journey around the Seven Wonders of the Ancient World.

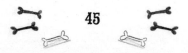

'I wonder why Lupton feels so confident about the whereabouts of the treasure?' Celia pondered. 'Maybe he found something in Ephesus after we'd left?'

'Distinctly possible,' said Satnam. 'I do have a worry that perhaps we gave up in Turkey too early.'

'Did we miss something? Are there any other possible sites close to the knight's library at Ephesus?' Celia asked.

Satnam looked at their list. 'The Tomb of Mausolus at Halicarnassus,' he said. 'It stood in a place now called Bodrum.'

Celia searched on her laptop. 'That's about a hundred miles from Ephesus. Here, look at the map.' She tilted the screen towards Satnam.

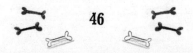

'Bodrum is on the coast, but so was Ephesus two thousand years ago,' said Dr Ghatak. 'The Avenger could have sailed between the two in little more than a day. We should go!'

Celia and Satnam explained their thoughts to Edith, who agreed that this was worth checking. There would be no beautiful steam train this time, so they would fly to Turkey as soon as they could. Destination: the Tomb of Mausolus.

Early the next morning Satnam and Celia set off for the airport. At the HQ of the Good Team, things were beginning to happen. Aisha sat in front of a mirror that Julimus had brought down from the shop floor. Edith had spent much of her life as a theatrical make-up artist

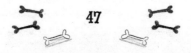

and was busy transforming Aisha from a girl into a young waiter.

'What's a gentlemen's club?' Aisha asked as Edith worked.

'Well, there are lots of them in London,' replied Edith. 'I used to walk past Lupton's club every day when I worked at the theatre. It was somewhere for *English gentlemen* only ... Rather terrifying, if you ask me.'

'It doesn't sound terrifying,' said Aisha. 'Isn't everyone there just a bit posh?'

'That's probably true these days,' replied Edith, 'but it is not the whole story. Nowadays the word *gentleman* means being polite and treating people in a respectful manner.'

'Like if you hold a door open for someone?'

said Aisha, who was enjoying seeing how her disguise was taking shape in the mirror.

'Exactly,' said Edith, pulling out a fake moustache. 'However, originally the word *gentleman* was used to describe the very rich. In those days, all gentlemen were part of the elite, high up in society. It was gentlemen that owned all the land and they lived off rent paid by peasants, who worked for them.'

'That doesn't sound very fair,' said Aisha.

'It wasn't,' agreed Edith. 'These gentlemen's clubs were somewhere these super-rich men could socialise, away from the masses. Just over a hundred years ago or so, women were not allowed to vote, neither were poor people. It was only gentlemen who voted.'

'Double not fair,' said Aisha.

'Women are not allowed to set foot in Lupton's club, Opulentos, even now.'

'That's why I have to have a moustache,' said Aisha.

'Yes,' said Edith. 'Now we just need a wig — and where did I put that waiter's costume Julimus found for you . . . ?'

Aisha looked at herself in the mirror and smiled. Edith was a skilful make-up artist and our hero's face was completely transformed.

4

Belling the Cat

By eleven o'clock the next morning, Aisha and Indiana were back in the centre of London. Mr Charman had phoned the kitchens at Opulentos earlier that morning, pretending to be part of their senior management team.

'I'm sending in a new waiter,' he had said

in his poshest, most severe voice. 'We have had complaints that the silver in the Reading Room is dull. I want the silver so bright in there today that our guests request sunglasses. Do I make myself crystal clear?' ... 'Yes, sir' had been the reply.

Now, Aisha was standing opposite Opulentos, dressed as a waiter. Her heart beating like a dormouse's at a disco, she studied the building. 'With a little bit of luck, this afternoon we could be back on the track of the treasure,' she whispered to Indiana.

Indiana looked up at his beloved pal. He knew that he would always do anything for her, but he was not feeling particularly excited. He'd been thinking about his mum again and

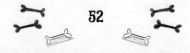

that had taken away some of his appetite for treasure hunting.

Opulentos was beautiful. The four-storey building was brilliant white, with huge double doors set back behind a grand entrance of marble pillars, which reminded Aisha of the ancient city of Ephesus, where she had last seen the slippery Serpent in the flesh. Heart still fluttering, she and Indiana carefully crossed the road.

Aisha swallowed hard and stepped through the large double doors. Indiana was still at her side but invisible now, strapped under our hero's magic shield. They stood for a moment in the main hall, which, as you might imagine, was super-grand. There were more

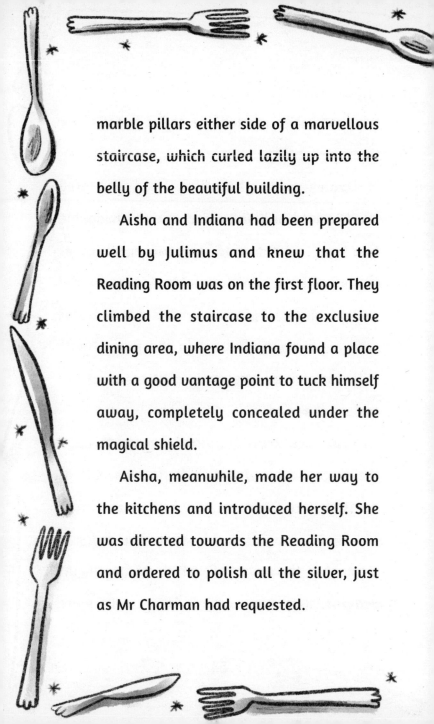

marble pillars either side of a marvellous staircase, which curled lazily up into the belly of the beautiful building.

Aisha and Indiana had been prepared well by Julimus and knew that the Reading Room was on the first floor. They climbed the staircase to the exclusive dining area, where Indiana found a place with a good vantage point to tuck himself away, completely concealed under the magical shield.

Aisha, meanwhile, made her way to the kitchens and introduced herself. She was directed towards the Reading Room and ordered to polish all the silver, just as Mr Charman had requested.

Armed with a bright white tea towel, our hero slowly made her way around the room, carefully lifting and polishing the silver knives, forks and spoons that had been laid out on the gleaming white tablecloths. The room was large and quiet and felt like a cross between a restaurant, a library and a stately home. Lunch guests began to arrive and take their seats, while waiters glided in and out. Aisha did her job well, and almost all the room's silver sparkled and gleamed. She looked at an antique clock on one of the many mantelpieces. It was one minute to twelve.

As Big Ben began to strike midday, into the Reading Room swept Lupton. He took a seat at his usual table, in the darkest, coolest corner, and summoned a waiter with a cold click of his fossilised fingers.

'Too bright,' he hissed softly, voice dripping with money, menace and malevolence. The nearest waiter knew the importance of this particular guest and moved swiftly to close some of the blinds. Several of the other diners were clearly not impressed by the blocking of the sunshine, but there was something about the ice-cool Serpent that made them continue with their own business quietly and without fuss. It was obvious to everyone in the room who was top of the food chain in this vulgar ecosystem.

Aisha shuddered but kept polishing at a safe distance, making her way methodically

around the room, doing her best not to be noticed. She felt for the bug in her pocket and was reassured to touch the tough, plastic casing of Celia's smallest listening device.

As Aisha worked, Indiana did too. He moved at the speed of a teenage tortoise, edging closer to Lupton, sliding on his belly under the shield, closer and closer, like a Bengal tiger silently stalking his supper.

The Serpent was served a glass of chilled champagne and he unfolded a newspaper and began to scan its pages while he waited for his first course. Sir Henry Lupton had been visiting this club ever since his father had first brought him on the day he turned twenty-one. The Serpent was a creature of habit with little

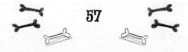

imagination, and had always had the same meal since that very first visit.

Aisha had planned with Edith exactly what to do. She worked her way around the room until she was next to Lupton. Taking the bug in her right hand, she fake-stumbled and spilled champagne all over his table. 'I'm terribly sorry,' she said in a fake boy's voice, as she attempted to mop up the spillage with a napkin.

She was about to reach around the seated Lupton and clip the bug to his jacket collar when Lupton seized her wrist.

'What are you doing, you idiot boy?' he fumed. 'Everyone here knows that it is strictly forbidden to approach me!'

'I'm sorry!' squeaked Aisha, shocked at his aggressive behaviour. 'You're hurting me!'

'Rule one: nobody comes within a metre of me. Rule two: nobody talks to me,' growled the Serpent.

Indiana Bones wanted to growl too, and was ready to pounce if necessary.

Lupton squeezed Aisha's wrist again, then sharply let it go. Disaster, dear readers! The bug flew out of her hand and landed under the table.

'Hang on a second,' said the Serpent. 'I know you.'

'No, sir,' replied Aisha, rubbing her wrist. 'I'm new.'

'I recognise you, boy — except you're not a boy, are you?' Lupton leaned over Aisha and

ripped her wig off. 'You're that ghastly Ghatak girl! Come to spy on me, have you?'

Up close, Lupton was even more terrifying. He looked like an impeccably dressed pterodactyl in his expensively tailored suit. He had the eyes of a shark, which he trained coldly on Aisha. 'Trying to bug me, no doubt. Well, you messed that up. Show me your hands!'

Aisha opened her empty hands and the villain snorted. Sitting down again, he lifted the tablecloth. There was nothing on the floor – except a bread roll someone had forgotten to sweep up. Lupton returned his shark eyes to Aisha.

'Well, let me save you Ghataks the trouble of eavesdropping on my conversations. I shall

60

tell you exactly what's what. I know where the treasure is. My brilliant father came within a whisker of finding it fifty years ago. Rest assured, I shall complete his life's work within the week.'

'You are one of the richest men in Britain. You don't need the treasure,' Aisha said boldly. 'Why the obsession?'

'It's not about the treasure, you stupid little girl. There is something else the Avenger found that I very much require. Something that will make the riches of the treasure seem like a penny in a puddle. Dark magic and history, ghastly Ghatak – dark magic and history. Now, get out of here before I have you thrown out.'

Before Aisha could move, Lupton seized her wrist again. 'Keep away from me. Or next time we meet I shall introduce you to the Grandmas, and they care less than I do about behaving badly in public, if you know what I mean.'

Aisha couldn't stand it any more. She wrenched herself free and ran out of the restaurant, all the way downstairs to the front entrance, where Indiana was waiting for her. He handed her back the shield, which she threw over her shoulder, then they raced outside and escaped into the sunshine.

They ran and ran until they reached the safety of a park several streets away, where Aisha finally broke down and sobbed. 'He's

horrible and scary and it's all gone wrong. I mucked it up.'

'No, Aisha,' said her friend. 'It may not have gone to plan, but you didn't muck it up. You were brave and you distracted him.'

Aisha blinked her tears away and stared at Bones, who was looking very pleased with himself.

'What did you do?' she asked.

Indiana grinned. 'I found the bug you dropped and fixed it to his shoe. He didn't feel a thing!'

Aisha gave her dog a big and slightly soggy hug. 'Who's my clever pal?'

They didn't celebrate for long. Things were better than Aisha had feared, but she was still shaken and worried.

'He knows where the treasure is and it's somehow linked to his father,' she said. 'And there's something else. Something to do with dark magic. We need to get back and warn the others. Come on!'

With that, our heroes ran out of the park and in the direction of Paddington train station.

5

Grandmas Have Entered the Chat

It was late afternoon when Aisha and Indiana arrived back at Charman and Dukes. Still shaken from their scarifying meeting with the Serpent, they breathlessly recounted their ordeal. Aisha felt as though the team was in a stew with a pickle on top. They seemed so far behind their nemesis in the search for the lost treasure of the Lonely Avenger.

'Have faith, Aisha. You did your job well and Indiana belled the cat!' said Edith, placing a steadying hand on her young friend's shoulders. 'Next comes a well-earned snack with a side order of patience.'

Edith was as wise as seventeen owls and she knew that things always felt better after a big plate piled high with hot buttery crumpets.

Q) Was she right, dearest book munchers?

A) Of course she widdley was.

As Indiana and Aisha chomped through their buttery feast, Julimus popped his head around the door. 'Well done, you two. Good news – the bug is working!'

This brought the beginnings of a smile to Aisha's face.

'Has he said anything useful?' Indiana asked through a particularly delicious mouthful.

'Not yet,' replied Julimus. 'He is in his office, listening to opera. It sounds as though he is on his own. All we can do is wait and see.'

'Wait and listen, more like,' chuckled Edith. 'Let's go and eavesdrop properly.'

'He was so horrible.' Aisha shuddered at the memory of him, as they headed through the

secret bookcase and down the steep stone steps towards the Good Team's nerve centre.

'You were brave to go,' said Julimus. 'I'm not sure that I could have done it.'

'Remind me again what he told you,' Edith said.

'It's a bit of a blur,' said Aisha. 'I just wanted to get out of there, to be honest.'

'He did say the thing about there being something dark and magical that was more important than the treasure,' said Indiana. 'And he said his father had been within a whisker of finding the treasure fifty years ago.'

'Now, that's interesting!' said Edith, turning to Julimus. 'See if you can find out what Horatio Lupton was up to fifty years

ago. Where he went, who he met, anything at all.'

A little later, they were joined by Mr Charman and Mr Dukes, who were ready to report back about their research into the Grandmas.

'Tell us what you've found out,' said Edith, pouring more tea.

'Well, our friend who used to work at the *Sunday Times* had quite a lot of information,' began Mr Dukes, pulling up a chair. 'But it's all rather scrappy, I'm afraid.'

'We took notes,' said Mr Charman, taking out a small leather-bound book from his inside jacket pocket. 'Apparently the identity of the Grandmas has been baffling police across Europe for more than a hundred years.'

'Gosh. A hundred years? I wasn't expecting that,' said Edith.

Mr Dukes continued. 'The first report was in Czechoslovakia, just after the end of the First World War, when a pair of bandits, calling themselves *Babičky*, held up a train and made off with more than a million pounds. It made them rather famous in criminal circles.'

'What is *Babičky*?' asked Aisha.

'Czech for "grandmas",' said Mr Charman, looking over his spectacles.

'Some say that they were twin brothers who were kicked out of the army during the First World War,' said Mr Dukes.

'But that would make them more than a hundred years old,' said Edith.

'Maybe they're ghosts?' joked Aisha.

'Interesting you should say that,' said Mr Dukes. 'Some reports say the brothers had dabbled in witchcraft and could live for ever.'

'Nonsense and poppycock,' said Edith. 'And I don't believe in ghosts either.'

'Over the following decades, the shadowy Grandmas cropped up all over Europe, from Reykjavik to Rome, Paris to Pompei,' continued Mr Dukes. 'It seems as though everybody was terrified of them.'

Indiana lay down and put his paws over his ears. He did not like the sound of the Grandmas.

Mr Charman joined in. 'They became legends. Figures of fear. The sort of thing

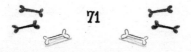

parents warned their children about when they wanted them to behave.'

'There are a great many more snippets about them,' added Mr Dukes, reading from his little book.

- They kidnapped and held to ransom a dozen elephants from the Moscow State Circus.

- They stole an entire train belonging to Queen Elizabeth II, right under the noses of the British Transport Police.

- The Grandmas held lavish parties for the criminal gangs of Europe in the castles and the palaces of the wealthy while they were on holiday,

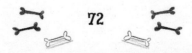

stripping them of their valuable contents when they were done.

- There had been a headline in a Spanish newspaper that the Grandmas were planning to steal the moon.

'And there is **STILL** a reward of one million pounds for information leading to their capture!' he finished.

'This all sounds like babble, balderdash and baloney,' said Edith, shaking her head. 'Are there no photographs of them?'

'Only one report of an actual sighting,' said Mr Charman. 'Fifty years ago, they were arrested and held in the Tower of London.

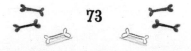

By morning they had escaped from a locked cell and the guard's hair had turned white overnight – with fear.'

At this, Indiana imagined his shaggy coat turning white and he let out a little whimper.

Suddenly Mr Charman and Mr Dukes's report was interrupted by gentle Julimus. 'Listen up! Lupton is making a telephone call.'

At his laptop, Julimus made a couple of clicks with his mouse and, hey presto, over the room's loudspeaker system, our team heard a phone ringing.

'Quiet, everyone,' whispered Edith. 'We don't want to miss a thing.'

After what seemed like an eternity, the phone was answered, and they heard

Lupton's voice. 'Hello, I wish to speak to the Grandmas.'

Silence. Then . . .

'Everybody wants to speak to the Grandmas,' came the cold reply. 'This is Good Grandma. Bad Grandma is here also. Speak.'

'I am travelling abroad and require new bodyguards,' Lupton said. 'You may also need to get rid of some nuisances for me. Two muddy archaeologists and their dumb dog.'

The soft hair along the ridge of Indiana's back bristled from his head to his tail and he growled quietly.

'Abroad is no problem. We get rid of nuisances all over the world,' said Good Grandma. 'But we are very expensive.'

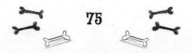

'Money is not an issue,' replied Lupton. 'Let us meet in Paris tomorrow. I shall be in touch with details.' And with that the line went dead.

Julimus closed his laptop and turned to his friends. 'Well, well, well,' he said, pleased. 'We now have some very good intelligence.'

'Excellent bugging,' agreed Edith, with a kind nod to Aisha and Indiana.

'So, that was the voice of a Grandma,' continued Julimus.

Indiana felt a second shiver run down his spine. 'That voice sure sounded real enough to me.'

'Right,' announced Edith, clapping her hands and moving everyone along. 'Paris! Aisha and Indiana, we have your next move.'

Aisha felt a mixture of terror and excitement bubbling inside her. She was frightened by the thought of the Grandmas, but there was nothing more wonderful than the thrill of being back on the hunt.

'Satnam and Celia need to head to Paris as soon as possible,' said Edith. 'And Dimitar Vakondember should be diverted to meet you there too. This calls for a full-team effort.'

Aisha and Indiana both felt relieved at the idea of some grown-up help. The Serpent and the Grandmas added up to a rather spooky combination, they thought.

'I wonder if our French knight may have hidden his famous fortune a little closer to home than we previously imagined. Home is

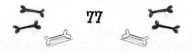

where the heart is after all,' said Edith, her
eyes twinkling.

'Maybe!' said Aisha, jumping up
and clapping.

**I hid the treasure in the best place in
the world.**

'That's what the knight said to me. It makes
sense. Home *is* the best place in the world! He
took his treasure back home to France!'

'Julimus,' Edith called out, 'your noodle just
got bigger and your haystack just got smaller.
Continue your search on Horatio Lupton but
focus on Paris.'

Indiana sat up rather wearily, his treasure

battery at zero per cent. He agreed about the home and the heart, and he realised he longed to visit his *first* home, the home of his mum in Skara Brae. As his friends chatted about Paris, Indiana felt the blue gemstone in his collar begin to glow softly. This felt like a strong sign that Paris was the place they should be looking. He would trust the sapphire and his friends, and recharge his treasure battery. Maybe after that he could persuade somebody to accompany him to Skara Brae.

There was a crackle of excitement in the air at Charman and Dukes as the elderly gentlemen of travel began sorting out tickets.

'I will contact Satnam and Celia,' said Edith.

'The Serpent may be about to slither out from underneath his stone.'

The search for the lost treasure of the Lonely Avenger was cranking up again. Little did the Good Team know that what they would find in the French capital would blow this clattering gladventure sky-high.

6

Agnes Swagness

The following morning Indiana and Aisha took yet another early train to London, where they caught the Eurostar to Paris. The team back in Oxford planned to keep track of them using the GPS on Aisha's phone and would be in regular contact. Our heroes would be joined as soon as possible in the French capital by some reassuring adults: her father and Celia, and hopefully Mr Dimitar Vakondember from the Bureau of Missing International Artefacts.

As regular as a clockwork cockerel, the swish Eurostar train slipped into the Gare du Nord in the centre of Paris. Aisha and Indiana travelled light, with just a ~~jetpack~~ backpack and the battered old shield between them. They left the train and hurried down the crowded platform. Aisha loved this journey and she felt better, more like her old self, confident and at ease.

Leaving the station, our heroes headed west towards the hotel that Edith had booked for them. As they walked, Indiana noticed a

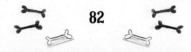

poster written in French. At the end of their previous gladventure, the Lonely Avenger had gifted Indiana the ability to read in many languages, something he never tired of using to impress Aisha.

'*Pickpockets in this area*,' he read aloud. '*Beware.*'

Aisha glanced at the poster, which showed a grainy photo of a child who looked like a cross between Peter Pan and a scruffy pixie.

'I'm not a wealthy none-of-your-businessman – I think I'll be okay,' said Aisha, grinning down at her canine companion. 'And you certainly don't need to worry; you don't have any pockets to pick.'

'True.' Indiana grinned back at her, feeling

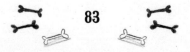

a big surge of love towards his number-one side-pal.

While Aisha consulted the map, our hairy hero trotted along happily, saying things like 'Oooh, that looks nice' at every single sandwich or cake shop they passed. After Indiana had stood on his hind legs, licked his lips and rubbed his belly for the tenth time, Aisha relented and went to get them several delicious treats from a patisserie, putting them in her backpack for later. Then, checking the map once more, Aisha decided to take a shortcut through a large market.

After a while, Aisha paused to look around.

'Confuzzled?' Indiana asked.

'Confirmative,' replied Aisha. 'I think we've

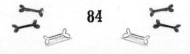

taken a wrong turn. Let's snack and work out where we are when our bellies aren't empty.'

As they sat and unpacked their lunch, the ancient, magical sapphire in Indiana's collar and the sapphire that hung around Aisha's neck began to glow softly.

'Something is about to happen,' said Indiana. His voice was quiet but urgent.

Our heroes worried that the Serpent was nearby, so Indiana's keen eyes scanned every inch of the market while they ate. There was no sign of Lupton, but he did spot someone he recognised.

'Look,' said Indiana. 'It's the kid from the poster.'

The tufty-haired urchin was walking

past a fruit stall and casually picked up an apple and a banana without paying for them. Glumfortunately for her, the market trader saw what had happened and gave chase, shouting.

Aisha knew that stealing was not right, but she also felt sorry for anyone who had to take food because they were unable to pay for it.

As they watched, the small incident began to grow into a big drama. A nearby policeman heard the hullabaloo and joined the chase, shouting urgently into his radio for assistance. The scene became even more chaotic as the chasing market trader knocked over a neighbouring fruit stall, sending apples and oranges flying around the square. The policeman slipped on the fruit and struggled to stay upright as he pursued the young girl. This was the most excitement the market had seen in years, and stall holders and other passers-by stopped what they were doing to watch and cheer.

There was a collective gasp as the young girl shinned up the drainpipe of a pink-shuttered, creamy-coloured building opposite Aisha and Indiana. Everybody clapped and whistled as the girl reached the rooftop.

'Any crowd loves an underdog,' whispered Indiana.

The girl was, it seemed, something of a performer, and she began waving at the

crowds, eating her apple while mock-curtseying and flexing her muscles in appreciation of the applause.

The policeman below scratched his head and called for more backup. Within moments the tables turned for our cheeky thief as about fifteen more police officers arrived. Several positioned themselves at each end of the market in an attempt to trap her. The rest set off into the building to find and flush out the fluffy little fruit fiend.

The girl looked down and assessed the situation. Then, to the amazement of Aisha and Indiana, she did the strangest thing: she began to howl at the sky.

How-how-howl

Howwwwl-howwwwl-howwwwl

How-how-howl

'What's she doing?' Indiana asked. 'She sounds like a wild animal.'

'I think I know,' said Aisha, her eyes dancing with excitement, 'and it's rather clever. I'm pretty sure that's Morse code. She's calling for help.'

How-how-howl

Howwwwl-howwwwl-howwwwl

How-how-howl

The crowd gave a collective '*Ooooh*' as three police officers arrived on the roof. It looked

as though the thief had run out of options, but she had other ideas. She stood and set off at speed, running like an Olympic sprinter, across the top of the building. Was she going to jump? Surely not! The gap between the buildings was far too big. She would never make it. At the building's end, she skidded to a halt.

Quick as a fla (*which is even quicker than a flash*), our speedy street sausage pulled a cable out of her backpack and threw it like a lasso across the gap between the buildings. The loop hooked over the top of a drainpipe. She fastened the other end to a drainpipe on her side and pulled it tight. Then, as if she wasn't several storeys up in the air with no safety net,

she strolled across the tightrope she had made to the next-door building.

The police dashed towards her, but the street kid, cooler than a snowman with sunglasses and a saxophone, unhooked the rope. With a deft flick of her wrist, she sent a wave along the wire, which lifted it off the drainpipe on the other building. As the officers watched, helpless, the world's swaggiest fruit burglar wound up her cable, put it back in her bag and began to walk away, calling out across the city once more:

How-how-howl

Howwwwl-howwwwl-howwwwl

How-how-howl

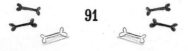

Aisha had been right about the SOS call. Suddenly dozens more street kids flooded the marketplace, howling hellos. The banana bandit slithered down another drainpipe and joined her friends in a great big mass at one end of the market. Then, as if by magic, the thief blended into the crowd and – *pff* – she disappeared.

The army of street muffins dispersed into various side streets as quickly as they had arrived, and when the police finally descended from the roof, there was no sign of them. Everyone in the market was completely confuzzled.

'Did you see where she went?'

'No, did you?'

'I didn't.'

'I swear she just ... disappeared.'

Not a single person knew how the girl had vanished so completely – but one animal did, and that animal was Mr Indiana Bones. 'Come on,' he whispered to Aisha. 'I think I've rumbled our friend. Let's go and say hello.'

As the market began to get back to business, our heroes left the hustle and bustle for the side streets. Indiana, sniffing at the ground, stopped abruptly. 'Here,' he said. 'Wait.'

They hid in a doorway halfway up the deserted street.

'What are we doing?' asked Aisha.

'Biding our time,' said Indiana, his sapphire

glowing gently. 'I think I know what is about to happen.'

A metre or so away, a manhole cover in the middle of the road jiggled and wriggled and lifted slowly, and a pair of brown eyes peered out. With the coast clear, the girl they'd watched evade capture so skilfully pulled herself out of her hiding place and into the sunshine. She dusted herself down, replaced the manhole cover and began to walk towards them, unaware that they were watching her.

As she passed, Aisha called out, 'Hey, hello there. Fantastic escaping!'

The little girl looked at them coolly. 'English?' she said.

'Yes,' said Aisha, adding, 'That was wonderful, by the way.'

The girl just stared back at her.

'We're lost,' said Aisha, not knowing quite what else to say. 'Can you help us find our hotel?'

The girl didn't reply.

'We can give you a pastry if you're hungry,' said Aisha, smiling and trying to look as friendly as a dolphin in a bobble hat.

'Sure,' replied the girl.

Aisha handed her a pain au chocolat from her backpack. 'We're staying at the Hotel Migny. Do you know where it is?'

'I know where everything is,' said the girl, before taking a big bite of pastry and setting

off. '*Allez*,' she said, which was French for 'Let's go'.

Five minutes later, the trio turned into a beautiful tree-lined street and stood outside a cafe on the corner. The cafe smelled so deliciously of hot chocolate that Indiana thought he may have to lie down and sniff it for all eternity. He snuffled at the smell longingly, as their new friend pointed across the road.

'L'Hôtel Migny,' she said.

'Thank you very much,' said Aisha.

'Your dog looks like he would like some hot chocolate,' said the girl.

'Oh, he's not allowed chocolate.' Aisha smiled. 'He does love the smell of it though.

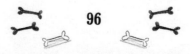

He will probably go for a milkshake. Let me get you a hot chocolate as a thank you for helping us. I'm Aisha, by the way, and this is Indiana Bones.'

Indiana rather liked their cool new friend and gave her a friendly tail wag like a normal dog, although really he wished he could stand on his hind legs, hold out a paw and say, 'Charmed I'm sure.'

'Okay,' said the girl. 'I am Agnes.' She pointed at another one of the pickpocket posters that was fixed to a lamp post nearby. 'There I am, or maybe it's one of my friends. We are wanted all over the city for trying to feed ourselves, but, as you know, it is not easy to catch us.' She smiled for the first time.

'Very true!' said Aisha, holding the cafe door open for Agnes. 'You were so awesome. I'm going to call you Agnes Swagness.'

Inside the cafe, they soon had big steaming bowls of French hot chocolate. Aisha ordered some croissants too, which they dipped in their drinks and munched as they chatted.

Agnes Swagness looked at Indiana. 'I like your dog,' she said. 'He thinks he's a human, doesn't he?'

Indiana raised a solitary eyebrow as he slurped his milkshake.

'Oh, you don't know the half of it,' replied Aisha. 'Where do you live, Agnes?'

'Everywhere. Nowhere,' replied Agnes. 'I don't have a proper home. One day I will

98

though. I'm going to open a home for all the street kids. It's my mission.'

Aisha did not know quite what to say. She thought about the Avenger's words:

I hid the treasure in the best place in the world.

Home. She wondered what it must be like to not have a home. She couldn't imagine it and felt terrible.

Agnes's revelation made Indiana feel bad too. He had a lovely home in Oxford, yet all he could think about lately was his first home in Skara Brae. But did this mean he had two homes, while Agnes didn't even have one?

He rested his chin on her lap and she stroked his back.

Ever the archaeologist, Aisha dug a little deeper. 'You must stay somewhere?' she persisted.

'Of course,' said Agnes Swagness. 'We live in the *Invisible City*. It's not nice, but it is safe and dry.'

'What's the Invisible City?' said Aisha.

'Don't ask – it will give you nightmares,' said Agnes, giving Indiana's ears a last ruffle before standing up awkwardly. 'Thanks for the hot chocolate. It was nice.'

Aisha worried that she'd asked too many questions and had frightened her new friend away. 'Before you go, take this,' she said. She

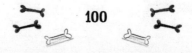

reached into her backpack and pulled out one of the jewel-encrusted keys. 'It might be worth something. You could sell it.'

'I can't,' said Agnes. 'It's yours.'

'Don't worry – I have two,' Aisha said, pulling out the other one to show her. 'I stole them from the world's most horrible man. He would absolutely hate you to have it, so you'd be doing me a favour.'

'Well, if you're sure,' said Agnes, almost smiling again. 'Thank you.' She waved the key at them. 'Maybe this could be the key to our new house!'

Then Agnes Swagness walked out of the cafe into the French funshine.

7

1952

Back in Oxford, down in the *shhhsecret* room below Charman and Dukes, Aisha and Indiana's backup team were working round the clock, searching for any slivers of slimportant funformation that might help our heroes on their quest.

'So,' said Edith Ellinor, stretching and standing up from her desk, 'where are our muffins?'

Julimus quickly checked Aisha's GPS history on his laptop. 'Well, they have booked into their hotel,' he replied.

'Are they still there?' Edith asked.

'Looks like it,' Julimus answered, tapping a couple of keys. 'It seems as though she's used a cashpoint and visited what looks like a cafe.'

'Good. Full bellies,' said Edith. 'It's important to eat. Let's hope it was delicious,' she added with a twinkle in her eye. She turned to the elderly gentlemen of travel. 'Mr Dukes and Mr Charman, what do you have?'

'Satnam and Celia fly into Paris today. As does Mr Vakondember, we hope — although he has proved hard to get hold of. His transport is, er, a little more erratic. We have yet to receive confirmation from him,' said Mr Charman.

'Good — some help, at least, is on its way,' said Edith. 'Where is Lupton?'

'The tracker on his shoe is still working well. We have him in Paris too,' said Julimus, looking at his laptop. 'He met with two unknown people this morning.'

'Almost certainly the Grandmas,' said Mr Dukes.

'Oh dear, that is a little worrying,' said Edith. 'And what news of your noodle and your haystack, Julimus?'

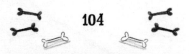

'I have run a hundred different searches for Horatio Lupton in Paris in every month of every year in the nineteen fifties,' he replied. 'But there is nothing useful.'

'Bother,' said Edith, perplexed. 'Nothing at all?'

'The odd mention,' said Julimus. 'In Paris there are references to him at auction houses, buying expensive works of art, and he crops up in the south of France on the guest lists of exclusive aristocratic parties. He rented a mansion right next to the Eiffel Tower for six months in 1952. I've studied all the articles in great detail, but have found nothing that helps us.'

'The fact that he lived in Paris in 1952 is intriguing though,' commented Mr Dukes.

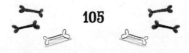

'Have you tried searching "Lonely Avenger" or "treasure in Paris" for 1952?' asked Edith.

Julimus nodded. 'I did. Nothing.'

'Okay. Back to basics,' said Edith, pacing. 'What do we know about Horatio Lupton?'

'Well, he was the original Serpent,' said Mr Dukes. 'It was a name he revelled in – he was a very boastful man.'

'When we followed Lupton after the war, the trail went cold, do you remember?' added Mr Charman. 'It was around that time that he started referring to himself as the Serpent instead of his real name. I think he rather liked how dangerous it made him sound.'

'Try "Serpent, Paris, 1952",' said Edith.

Julimus began to type. Moments later his

eyes widened. 'Oh my goodness, Edith. This looks interesting. Let me enlarge it.' He made a couple of mouse-clicks and displayed the front page of a British newspaper.

LE PATRON

PARIS SERPENT TERROR

Reports of an enormous serpent terrorising tourists at one of Paris's top tourist attractions have led to police closing the famous Catacombs until further notice. Visits to the labyrinth beneath the French capital are forbidden while police search the

200 miles of tunnels and chambers for the monster.

Dating back to 1786, and known among locals as the Invisible City, the famous Catacombs are a complex network of passageways running for miles below the streets of Paris. The tunnels and chambers were used to store the bones of the deceased from overflowing cemeteries. The labyrinth is packed with more than six million skeletons and has long held a gruesome fascination for tourists and Parisians alike.

The panic started when an English tourist, Major Edward Marshall, sent a photograph to *Le Patron* of what he claimed to be a vast snake-like creature that he saw when visiting the Invisible City in January, sparking terror among traumatised tourists. The director of the Catacombs, Maurice Tatou, dismissed the photo, saying it was a trick of the light. He was not available for comment and has not been seen for several weeks. Rumours abound that he may have become a victim of the subterranean monster.

'I recognise that name!' gasped Mr Dukes. 'Major Edward Marshall was one of Horatio Lupton's close associates.'

'I don't understand,' said Julimus. 'Horatio Lupton was not a real serpent.'

'I can make a guess,' said Edith, her blue eyes dancing with new ideas. 'I think Horatio Lupton believed the treasure was hidden somewhere in the Catacombs but couldn't search them because of all the visitors, so he cooked up a story about a monster down there. He fakes a couple of stories of sightings, gets rid of the director, bribes a few policemen and the site is closed for six months.'

'Giving him time to search the whole area in peace,' said Mr Charman, nodding his head in agreement.

'But, crucially, he found nothing,' Edith continued. 'Fast-forward fifty years and our Lupton thinks his father may have been just

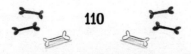

inches away from discovering the treasure.'

'Oh my,' said Mr Dukes solemnly. 'He is going back to finish what his father started.'

'We need to tell Aisha and Indiana immediately,' said Edith. 'They have to get there before Lupton does. Send Aisha the article, Julimus, and tell her to call us the very moment she's read it.'

The HQ of the Good Team was buzzing like a bee with a kazoo. Nobody could concentrate on anything until they heard from Aisha and Indiana. At last, Julimus's smartphone began to ring and Aisha and Indiana's excited faces appeared on screen.

'This is brilliant!' said Aisha. 'I don't know how you managed to dig it up. Well done!'

'Teamwork makes the dream work,' said Julimus, happy to see his young friends.

'It's the most amazing coincidence,' said Aisha, who was feeling slightly freaked out. 'We met a girl called Agnes who said she lives in the Invisible City. Six million skeletons! No wonder she didn't want to talk about it.' She turned to Indiana. 'Do you think we can find her again?'

'No time for that,' interrupted Edith. 'Lupton and the Grandmas are already in town. You must get there first. Your father, Celia and Dimitar are on their way. As soon as we can, we'll tell them to head to the Catacombs.'

'Ah. Okay,' said Aisha. 'What should we do when we get there?'

'Get yourselves on a tour of the Catacombs immediately,' Edith instructed. 'As soon as it's safe, sneak away from your party. There are several miles of passageways that are out of bounds to tourists – you must search every inch. If anyone can sniff out the treasure, Indiana can!'

'Confirmative,' said Indiana Bones, standing on his hind legs and saluting.

'All right then,' said Aisha, picking up her backpack and preparing to leave the hotel room. 'Anything else?'

'Yes,' said Edith. 'Indiana will not be allowed in with you. I suggest you take your snazzy shield to conceal him. I am sending a map of the Catacombs to your phone right now.

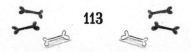

Oh, and take your brightest torch. It's going to be dark down there.'

8

The
Invisible City

Exactly fifty-seven minutes and thirty-two seconds later, and with the map downloaded, Indiana and Aisha arrived at the Catacombs. Indiana gulped. Our hairy hero was nervous.

He didn't mind the dark, but the dark with six million skeletons was a bit too spooktacular for comfort. Before our heroes joined the queue, Aisha strapped the invisibility shield to her beloved pooch's back. It worked a treat. Indiana was well and truly concealed.

The entrance to the city's most grisly attraction was unassuming – a small, dark green, windowless wooden entrance, with a kiosk to pay, and a door that led into a small stone building. It gave little away as to what would greet them below.

Inside, a simple staircase curled down into the subterranean labyrinth that was the Invisible City, home to more than a billion bones. It should have been a dog's wildest

dreams come true, but our hairy hero was shaking like an egg. His brave front had evaporated. 'I am really not looking forward to this,' he admitted quietly.

'Don't worry, ladoo. I'll look after you,' said Aisha.

Aisha waited patiently in line, but Indiana was as restless as a raincloud. Nerves had put our favourite four-legged friend in super-watchful mode. The sapphire in his collar was alive, glowing and pulsing, and the magical pooch knew for sure that someone, somewhere, was spying on them. He scanned the faces of everyone in the queue and studied passers-by, but, whoever it was, they were doing an excellent job of remaining hidden.

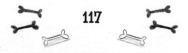

At last, the archaeolo-muffins reached the front of the queue and Aisha bought a ticket for the next tour. They shuffled along slowly in their little group, moving from sunshine to shadow. At the bottom of the stairs, their guide introduced herself as Sylvie Travert, a history student and expert in all things historic and undergroundy.

They made their way along a passage and down more staircases, which eventually delivered them to a large chamber – thankfully well lit with electric lights. The end of the chamber opened into a wide passageway and Aisha got her first glimpse of the famous skelebones lining the myriad tunnels and chambers.

Sylvie Travert paused the group here.

'Welcome, everybody. We are now twenty metres under the streets of Paris in the world-famous Catacombs, the final resting place of more than six million Parisians.'

Indiana gulped. Aisha slipped her hand under the shield and rested a reassuring hand on his hairy head.

Their guide continued. 'They were constructed to store the bones of the dead from the many cemeteries of Paris, which were, at the time, overflowing. At first the bones were just stored down here, but later the skeletons themselves were used to line the tunnels and chambers that we will see on our visit. Follow me, please . . .'

*

As they made their way through the bone-lined labyrinth, Aisha looked for somewhere she and Indiana could dip away from the crowd. A little further along they came across a doorway with more steps. It was roped off, with a sign reading:

ENTRÉE INTERDITE

'*Entry forbidden,*' Indiana whispered. 'Shall we?' he asked, hoping very much that Aisha would reply, *Definitely not. Let's go back up and have some more croissants in the lovely sunshine instead.*

'Looks like as good a place as any,' is what Aisha actually said, so she and Indiana snuck under the rope and down the stairs.

The deeper underground they headed, the chillier the air grew. The lights from the main tour were now far behind them, so Aisha pulled out her torch and shone it around. Indiana, having returned Aisha's shield, saw that they were in yet another skele-passage, and the walls were stuffed with hundreds of skulls, all of which looked as though they were staring at our heroes. Indiana gulped again.

Aisha looked at the bones. These had been real people once, just like her. It reassured her to think that they had been tailors, soldiers, merchants, shopkeepers, bakers, dancers, uncles and aunties, nephews and nieces. This made her mind boggle and she realised she was not thinking enough about the job at hand.

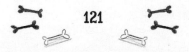

Pausing, she and Indiana checked the map that Julimus had sent. The passages and chambers all had strange names.

Tomb of the Giants

Large Soul of a Nameless Soldier

Tranquil Walk of Peace

Darkmoon Ring

Soul of a Lonely Knight

This last name caught Indiana's eye. 'Look, Aisha,' he urged. 'Surely that's the place to start.'

Aisha peered at the map. 'Typical that it's the furthest away!' she said. 'Why can't it be just next door so we can pop our heads around

the corner, see that it is empty and head up for a hot chocolate?'

'Confirmative,' Indiana agreed. 'This place is giving me the heebie-jeebies.'

Our heroes worked out that they were in the Tomb of the Giants and then planned the direction they needed to take. Calmly and methodically, they set off into the darkness.

Back at HQ, everybody was busy. Julimus was doing more research on the Catacombs, while Edith was attempting to ascertain the whereabouts of Satnam, Celia and Dimitar. As yet, she hadn't been able to reach any of them.

Even though their flight had been delayed, she was pretty sure that Satnam and Celia

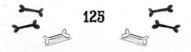

were in Paris, and she was keen that they get themselves to the city centre as soon as possible. Jovis was with his dad, Julimus, sitting on his knee and trying to track the whereabouts of Mr Dimitar Vakondember. The last time they'd spoken to him, he was having technical difficulties and had been forced to land somewhere in Austria. But they didn't know where he was now.

At a laptop below the blown-up photo of Sir Henry Lupton, Mr Charman and Mr Dukes were taking it in turns to keep an eye on the flashing red dot that marked the location of the tracker on the slithery Serpent.

'He's on the move,' Mr Dukes said suddenly.

Our team gathered around and watched

as the little red blinking dot began to move speedily towards the centre of Paris.

'He must be in a car,' Julimus observed.

'Look, we were right,' said Edith, as it became clear where the dot was heading. 'He's going to the Catacombs.'

'I can't help thinking that the fact that Lupton himself is on the move, no doubt accompanied by that smelly fool Ringo, is extremely significant,' remarked Mr Charman. 'Whatever is down there must be very important. What's changed?'

'Whatever it is, it's a worry,' agreed Edith. 'But we'll have to think about that later. Right now Aisha and Indiana are down in the Catacombs alone.'

'We must warn them!' said Julimus. 'What if Lupton has the Grandmas with him?'

'A young girl and a shaggy dog are no match for the gruesome Grandmas,' Mr Dukes concurred.

Julimus grabbed his phone, but the colour drained from his face as he said, 'Straight to voicemail.'

'Of course, she must be underground already,' groaned Edith. 'No reception.'

The Good Team stared at each other in horror. Our friends in Oxford were more than three hundred and fifty miles away from Aisha and Indiana. The grown-ups they hoped would be able to offer backup were, as yet, nowhere to be seen. As Lupton's face loomed

large above them, from his picture on the wall, things for Aisha and Indiana were not looking good, my friends. They were not looking good at all.

9

Lost Souls

Back in Paris, the queue for the Catacombs snaked past an ice cream stall. Close by were Sir Henry Lupton and his hired muscle, Ringo.

'Would you like an ice cream, sir?' Ringo asked his boss, thinking that would be a nice way to pass the time while they waited.

'No, I would not like an ice cream,' the Serpent hissed. 'I'm not six.'

The big guy blushed. For Ringo, there had never been much joy working for the unpleasant Serpent, but now that grumpy Philip Castle was out of the picture, all his boss's bad temper was focused on him. In the queue behind them were two men in black suits and bowler hats. Over the suits they wore long, sandy-coloured trench coats, and both carried old brown leather suitcases. The thing that made children stare and other tourists feel nervous was the fact that their faces were completely wrapped in white bandages. If there were holes for their eyes, no one could tell, because both were wearing very dark sunglasses.

Ringo glanced back at them quickly and sighed. There was no chance either of them would want an ice cream.

Down in the dark, bony underbelly of the French capital, Aisha and Indiana were unaware of the approaching danger. They did not know that Lupton and his cronies were right on their waggy tails, and of course they were completely clueless that fifty years ago Lupton's father had also been down here, probably also searching in the chamber known as the Soul of a Lonely Knight, the very place that they were heading to.

Aisha and Indiana wove in and out of the various bone-lined passageways. Even with the help of the map, occasionally they had to

retrace their footsteps having made a wrong turn. It helped having Indiana's hairy hooter on hand as he was quickly able to pick up their scent and snuffle them back on course.

Our subterranean superstars passed through the Tomb of the Giants and into the Large Soul of a Nameless Soldier. Here they paused to drink water and share a pastry to keep their spirits up and energy levels high.

They continued through the long slender passageway known as the Tranquil Walk of Peace and into a small circular chamber that Aisha thought must be Darkmoon Ring.

'I think the chamber we're looking for is through there,' said Aisha, shining the torch ahead.

'The Soul of a Lonely Knight,' said Indiana. 'What do you think we'll find?'

'Who knows?' Aisha replied. 'But I don't think it will be as simple as an enormous pile of treasure.'

'No,' agreed Indiana. 'Though I do predict the possibility of more bones.'

Aisha smiled down at Indiana. 'I wouldn't bet against it, my furry fruit flake.'

They made their way through Darkmoon Ring, buzzing with anticipation. As they walked along the connecting passageway into the Soul of a Lonely Knight, the air became chillier. The sapphires in Indiana's collar and Aisha's necklace began to glow brighter. Was it a sign they were close to the treasure? Or was danger

lurking just around the corner? Indiana was not sure, and he sniffed at the cold, dark air for any kind of clue.

'Do you smell anything?' Aisha asked.

'Skulls,' Indiana replied dryly.

'Let's definitely not split up,' said Aisha with a shudder.

'Confirmative,' said Indiana. 'Let's stick together like a pair of sticky stick insects who are also best friends and twins. I do not like it down here one bit.'

Aisha shone the powerful torch beam all around them. Indiana saw that the room they were in was vast, about the size of a football pitch. It looked like an underground quarry, with steep banks of limey-stoney rubble at the

edges, littered with (you guessed it, brilliant book munchers) even more bones.

They began to search the chamber. As Aisha scrabbled to the top of one of the mounds, in her head she apologised to all the people whose remains she was stepping on. *Excuse me, sir. Sorry, madam. I beg your pardon. Sorry to disturb you. Oops, apologies. Pardon me. Was that your bone? My bad ...* She hoped that if there *were* any ghosts down here, they would be able to tell that she was polite and respectful, and they'd leave her alone. So far, it was working.

Aisha and Indiana made a slow and methodical search around the perimeter. It took ages, and they didn't find anything that looked like it might be hiding treasure.

'I don't even know what we're looking for,' said Indiana at last.

'Well, I was hoping we'd find a door,' said Aisha. 'Somewhere we could use that key.'

'This feels like the last place you would find a door,' replied Indiana.

'I know,' said Aisha. 'I guess we've just got to keep looking for anything that looks strange or out of place.'

Our heroes continued to search carefully. This is what they found:

- Nothing.
- Nada.
- Nowt.
- Zero.

- Zilch.

- Zip.

They were now back to where they had started, with the passageway entrance to the chamber up a little bank above them.

'We're getting nowhere,' said Aisha eventually, pausing to sit on a boulder. 'Let's break for ten minutes and have a snack, then head back up and inform HQ. I don't think there's a solitary sausage down here for us.'

'Confirmative,' said Indiana, stretching out and resting a hairy chin on his best friend's feet. 'And I'm not just saying that because being down here makes me feel tenser than ten ticklish teapots.' He sighed. 'Having met the knight, I don't feel like this is the kind of place he would hide his treasure in. It's too spooky.'

'I know what you mean,' said Aisha. 'It's not a bit like the Lost Library. And I don't think anyone could call it the best place in the world.'

'More like the worst place in the world,' agreed Indiana Bones.

At that moment, Indiana's heart began to race and an awful but familiar smell wafted into his nostrils. He realised that the sapphire in his collar was now burning a deep electric blue and pulsing like the light on a police car.

A terrifying voice came out of nowhere.

'**Well, well, well.** Will you take a look at

this? If it isn't the ghastly little Ghatak worm and her disgusting dumb dog.'

Aisha and Indiana leaped to their feet. On the bank above them, at the entrance to the cavern, was the Serpent, Sir Henry Lupton. His stinky minion Ringo was at his side, shining a large light down on our fearful friends. Indiana knew at once that this was dangerous – their only way out was blocked.

Behind them stood two shadowy figures that Aisha couldn't quite see. They were holding large burning candles and the shadows they cast loomed and flickered menacingly on the limestone walls.

Aisha pretended to be far more courageous than she was feeling. She shone her torch up

at the group and shouted, 'If you're looking for the treasure, Lupton, don't bother. It's not down here.'

'It's *Sir* Lupton to you, grubby little mole,' replied the Serpent. 'Also, congratulations on placing the bug on my shoe. It's smashed to pieces now, but you and the revolting hound will pay dearly for that very soon.'

Aisha tried to give Lupton her coldest, bravest stare.

'And you are very much mistaken about the treasure's whereabouts,' Lupton continued. 'You and your pointless pooch are just too stupid to find the door concealed in this very chamber.'

Despite her fear, Aisha felt a throb of hope. 'Oh, right,' she said, trying to keep cool. 'And I

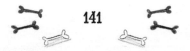

suppose all that treasure you're obsessed with is on the other side.'

'I already told you, you slug,' said Lupton. 'It's not about the treasure.'

'I remember,' said Aisha. 'But what's so important that you and your father have spent your whole lives looking for it? Is it the Holy Grail?'

'Better,' said Lupton, a lazy half-smile crossing his lizardy lips. 'Have you heard of the Sleeper of Ephesus, you grimy little rat? No, of course you haven't. Your father will have though. Let me enlighten you before we lock you down here for ever.'

Aisha and Indiana were torn. On the one hand, they wanted to sprint as fast as possible

and see if there was any other way out of the large chamber. On the other, they wondered what Lupton could be about to tell them. Stuck between a rock and a hard place, they had no choice for the moment, and so they just listened.

'There was once a man who became known in historical circles as the Sleeper of Ephesus — name of Marius. He was a mathematician and clockmaker who was in debt to the devil himself. As a repayment, the devil forced Marius to create, with the help of a master jeweller, something deliciously dark and wonderfully wicked. Its power was far too much for mankind. The devil hoped it would unleash havoc on the world. Frightened about

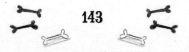

143

what he had made, Marius hid in a cave outside the city of Ephesus.'

'What did he make?' Aisha asked.

'It was a magical and powerful timepiece, fashioned out of gold and richly decorated with rubies,' Lupton replied. 'My father unearthed the story of it when I was but a boy. He became very keen that this timepiece should become part of our collection of interesting artefacts.'

There was something in the Serpent's slippery voice that gave Aisha the feeling that this story was not going to end well.

'On his return from the cave, Marius told a friend all about his deal with the devil. The friend betrayed him and Marius was

discovered. He was chased out of the city, but sneaked back the following day. Young Marius thought he had only been away from the city for a night but, feeble Ghatak, he had in fact been away for seven years. During his journey home, he had travelled in time, setting coordinates on his timepiece and dipping in and out of many different eras.'

'I don't much like the way that this is heading,' whispered Indiana.

Lupton continued, very much enjoying the sound of his own voice. 'Marius understood that with his invention he could go back and alter the course of history. Racked with guilt, he hid the timepiece somewhere in Ephesus. I believe that our knight, the Lonely Avenger,

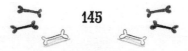

found the timepiece in Ephesus. Unaware of its importance, it simply became part of his treasure.'

'So what?' Aisha called up defiantly.

'Are you dim, girl? The timepiece we are talking about is called Dux Temporis, which translates as the time commander!' Lupton bellowed. 'Dux Temporis is here. I will use it to travel back in time. I shall alter history and ensure that the Lupton family is the wealthiest on the planet. I will own ninety-nine per cent of all the riches in the world. What's a paltry treasure hoard compared with that?' He stopped and looked deliciously pleased with himself.

Aisha and Indiana could not imagine

anything worse than a world controlled by Lupton.

'We will stop you,' was all Aisha could think to say.

'You will not,' said Lupton. 'You have been an irritation for far too long and it is time for you to be silenced.' He turned towards the flickering candlelight. 'Grandmas!' he commanded.

The air surrounding Aisha and Indiana began crackling with electricity, and then came a loud boom of thunder. They looked around but could see nothing. Next came the deafening whinny of horses, sounding as though they were almost on top of them.

'Let's get out of here!' Aisha shouted to Indiana. 'Quickly! There must be another exit!'

The pair sprang to their feet and sprinted across the large chamber. At the other end, Indiana spotted a small tunnel they hadn't noticed before. They headed for it at speed.

As they ran, more scary, strange noises followed them – whipping wind, lashing rain and a horrendous hubbub of horrible hooves. It sounded like the horses were frightened too, as terrified whinnies echoed through the labyrinth of passageways.

Our fearful friends turned a sharp left and raced down a wider passageway that sloped steeply downwards, their bright torch shining the way in front.

'We are completely lost now,' Aisha said as they raced on. 'How will we ever find our way out?'

'As long as we avoid what's behind us, I don't care,' replied Indiana.

Then came a sound so unexpected it almost made their hearts stop. A child's voice boomed: *'What big eyes you've got, Grandmama.'*

An old lady's voice replied: *'All the better to see you with.'*

The child's voice rang out again: *'What big ears you've got, Grandmama.'*

'All the better to hear you with,' came the reply.

Our heroes did not know what to make of these creepy voices, but they knew they didn't want to hang around and find out. Up ahead loomed a huge black space and they realised they were coming to a ledge. There was nowhere left to run!

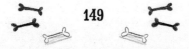

'*What big teeth you've got, Grandmama,*' said the child.

'*All the better to EAT YOU WITH!*'

Running faster than ever, Aisha and Bones reached the ledge and leaped as high and as far as they could. They flew through the dark, arms and legs flailing and pumping as if they were still running.

They landed with a crunch, breathing hard. From above, there was total silence. No voices, no hooves, no whipping wind.

'Aisha, are you okay?' asked Indiana.

'Confirmative,' Aisha replied, rubbing her knee. By some miracle, she still had hold of the powerful torch. She shone it around to see where they had landed. Readers, it

was not good news. They were on a ledge protruding from a large cliff face opposite and below the point they'd leaped from. I'm sorry to say that our heroes were well and truly stuck.

They sat in silence for a while. There was no sign that anyone had followed them – no Grandmas, no Serpent, no one. Then Aisha had an idea.

'Maybe the shield can help us,' she said to Indiana. 'There are three stones in it. One makes the shield invisible, and one makes the shield turn back to normal, but there's one I'm not sure about.'

'Show me,' said Indiana. Aisha shone the torch and Indiana saw the sapphire Aisha

was talking about, with the words **Invisibilia Videre** underneath.

'It's Latin, for "see the unseen",' Indiana translated. 'Maybe it's like our sapphires, Aisha. They warn us about things we cannot see, or what is to come.'

'Maybe if I press the sapphire, it will show us a way out that we can't see?' she suggested.

'Do it,' said Indiana. 'What have we got to lose?'

Aisha took a deep breath and covered the sapphire with her palm. From the shield's centre, a blue laser-like beam shot out into the darkness.

Aisha cast the beam around their cavernous

prison, but it didn't reveal any secrets. No way of escape. No new hope.

It was all too much for brave Aisha, who released her hand from the sapphire, killing its beam. She began to weep. 'Oh, Indiana, Lupton is going to find Dux Temporis and the whole world will be doomed, and we can't even get out to try to stop him. We'll end up as the skeleton of a girl and the skeleton of a dog stuck down here for ever, like all the other sad souls. What on earth are we going to do?'

10

You Should Always Keep in Touch With Your Friends

In the dark, deep underground below the streets of Paris, our heroes had reached rock-bottom

 154

in more ways than one. Their pursuers, it seemed, had disappeared almost as quickly as they'd appeared. Stuck on a ledge, all Aisha and Indiana could do was cuddle and comfort each other.

Unable to simply sit and do nothing, Aisha rooted through her backpack to see if she had anything that might help them. She pulled out a long climbing rope and a grappling hook, which she began trying to throw to a high ledge she'd spotted above them, but each time it fell agonisingly short.

Indiana sat up, excited by a sudden idea. 'I'm gonna call for help,' he said.

'Good luck,' said Aisha, trying to be encouraging, though on the inside she was

thinking, *Who on earth is going to hear us all the way down here?*

Indiana began his call:

How-how-howl

Howwwwl-howwwwl-howwwwl

How-how-howl

Our friends spent a desperate hour in this fashion: Aisha throwing and missing with the grappling hook; and Indiana Bones calling out into the dark as if their lives depended on it. Which, dearest book munchers, they kinda did.

How-how-howl

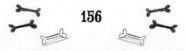

howwwwl-howwwwl-howwwwl

how-how-howl

Eventually Aisha was too tired to carry on. She sat down with a sigh. In the sudden quiet, Indiana froze.

'Did you hear that?' he said, ears pricked.

'No,' said Aisha through frustrated tears.

Indiana howled out once more and this time a quiet howl came back to him. 'You must have heard that?'

'Oh, Indiana, that was just the echo of your own howl,' said Aisha sadly.

'Aw, man!' said Indiana. Giving up too, he slumped to the floor and rested his chin on his paws.

They sat in silence, each wondering how long it would take to become a pile of dry, dusty bones in the deepest, darkest depths of the Catacombs.

Then, drifting through the cold air, they heard the faintest, tiniest sound.

How-how-howl

howwwwl-howwwwl-howwwwl

how-how-howl

They leaped up. Indiana howled back a reply. Sure enough, somebody or something responded. He called out again and again; each time the reply came back a little louder.

And then something wonderful happened:

a voice called to them from the ledge above. Aisha shone the torch upwards and there was the one and only Agnes Swagness looking down at them, with a big grin on her face.

'Are you two lost *again*?' she asked cheekily.

'Not any more!' said Aisha. 'Oh, Agnes, how did you find us?'

'I thought I would keep an eye on you after we left and so I followed you to the entrance of the Catacombs,' she replied.

I knew someone was watching us! Indiana thought to himself.

'Me and my friends live down here, but where we stay is miles away,' Agnes told them. 'I snuck down here through one of our secret entrances, but then I saw you weren't with the tour group.'

'You are now officially the greatest human in the universe,' Aisha said, beaming at her. 'Can I throw you my rope?'

Aisha lobbed the rope, minus the grappling hook, up to Agnes, which she caught first time. Everything, dearest book munchers, is easier when you have a friend. As Aisha scrambled up the cliff face, she was amazed at the strength of the young French girl, but when she reached the top, she got the shock of her life. It hadn't been Agnes pulling her up – it was Ringo! They stared at each other, and Aisha felt a pibble of panic. Was Agnes somehow part of the bad team now?

'Don't worry,' said Ringo. 'I'm here to help.'

'But I don't understand,' said Aisha. 'You were with Lupton.'

'After he'd set the Grandmas on you, he turned on me,' Ringo said glumly. 'He said I was a weak and worthless worm who would end up in the gutter where I belong, and that I was stupid and smelly.' The big man looked at the ground, embarrassed.

'I found him crying in the dark,' Agnes chipped in. 'I told him I was searching for a girl and her dog. He led me in the right direction – and then I heard your calls.'

Aisha looked at Ringo. He looked truly sad, a little boy unable to stand up to a bully. Like everyone else, Lupton had chewed him up and spat him out.

'It was kind of you to pull me up,' she said to him.

Agnes threw the rope down to Indiana, and Ringo, using just one arm, pulled him up too. Indiana was just as shocked to see their stinky adversary. Aisha shot Indiana a wink that meant she thought they could trust him.

'I wonder what happened to the Grandmas,' Aisha said.

'Who?' Agnes asked.

Aisha explained about the scariest men in the world who'd been galloping after them, and all the thunder and the rain, and the creepy voices.

'Oh, them,' said Agnes matter-of-factly. 'We locked them in a cupboard.'

Aisha stared at her, wide-eyed. 'Excuse me?'

'Me and Ringo locked them in a cupboard. Well, it's more than a cupboard. There's a room down here for all the electrics. We locked them in there.'

'What about their horses?' Aisha asked. She really was confused.

'There were no horses,' Agnes explained. 'They were using a recording and a loudspeaker, which they had in one of their suitcases. It's a trick. They're basically just two old men. When we were on our way here, we found them sniggering about chasing you off a ledge. So Ringo pushed them into the room and then pushed a very heavy rock in front of the door.'

'Wow,' said Aisha, feeling a mixture of

admiration for Agnes's awesome swagginess and embarrassment for how easily she and Bones had been fooled by the myth of the Grandmas.

Our relieved friends sat for a while in the lamplight and Aisha told Agnes all that had happened to them: about the treasure, the richly jewelled, terrifying, ticking timepiece Dux Temporis, and how they had searched in the Soul of a Lonely Knight for a door.

'Oh, I know that door,' said Agnes, cooler than a baby hedgehog in a bandana. 'It's locked. The street kids stay away from there. It feels a little bit ... well, scary.'

'Spooky,' said Aisha, shivering.

'Ha ha!' said Agnes, smiling. 'Spooooky!

That is a good word. The spooooky, spooooky door is not far from here. I can take you.'

Before long they were back in the chamber known as the Soul of a Lonely Knight.

'This way,' said Agnes, scrambling up a limestone bank. At the top were two big boulders, separated by the slimmest of gaps.

They all squeezed through, except for poor Ringo who was too large. 'I'll stand guard,' he said. 'Just in case.'

'Thank you,' said Aisha.

Once they'd squished through, what they saw took their breath away. It was a huge oak door, the kind that you would normally see inside a great hall or a castle. Aisha froze.

There was no need for the fancy key, because the door had been smashed to pieces and was hanging off its hinges.

Aisha groaned. 'Of course, the Serpent would have come straight here after we scarpered.'

The friends stepped through what was left of the door, Aisha with her torch and Agnes with her lantern. They found themselves in a grand stone-lined chamber. When they reached the far end, they arrived at a marble statue of a king in armour, wielding a sword. Next to the statue was an enormous, intricately carved stone that looked like some sort of map.

Caught up in the moment, Indiana pored

166

over the words at the statue's base, reading aloud: *'In honour of King Guntram the Great.'*

Agnes spun round. 'What?' she said to Aisha. 'Your dog who thinks he is a human is now talking like a human!'

'I know,' said Aisha, grinning. 'He does that sometimes. He's a little bit, sort of, magic.'

Agnes crouched and rubbed Indiana's ears. Our hero liked this and winked at his new friend.

'It's true,' he said. 'I am a little bit magic, but you need to keep me a secret. We don't want everyone to know.'

'Promise,' said Agnes Swagness.

Indiana explained to Agnes all about the Lonely Avenger. 'We thought his fortune might be down here, but it seems not,' he said.

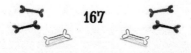

'You must not give up!' Agnes said to them. She was looking at the map next to the statue. 'Why have a map down here? It is strange, no?'

Aisha took a closer look and squealed with excitement. Pointing at the bottom of the map, she said, 'Look, Indiana! It's the Avenger's mark and some writing. He's left us another clue. Can you read it?'

Indiana looked at the words:

QUAERITE ANTRUM MARIS

'What does it mean?' Aisha asked.

Indiana Bones studied the words. The answer was on the tip of his tongue but

168

somehow remained just out of reach. He couldn't work it out. 'I'm not sure,' he finally said.

'Well, it's a map of North Africa and Europe,' said Agnes. 'If that's where your treasure is, bad luck. It's a very big area to search.'

'Maybe there are some clues hidden somewhere in the map,' said Aisha. 'Let's photograph it and get out of here. Maybe Julimus will be able to find something useful.'

Indiana and Agnes looked a little crestfallen, but Aisha was upbeat. 'Don't you see?' she said. 'All is not lost – the treasure isn't here, which means that Lupton doesn't yet have the ticking time-bomb that is Dux

Temporis. We're still in with a chance of stopping the Serpent. We may still be able to save the *world*!'

11

Into the Light

With Agnes Swagness as their leader, it wasn't
long before our dusty team was clambering up
a long metal ladder, popping another manhole
cover and emerging out of the darkness of
the Catacombs into the wonderful blinky
French funshine.

They surfaced in a small park called Square Claude-Nicolas-Ledoux. As soon as they were all out, they flopped back onto the grass and let out a huge sigh of relief. It had, beloved book munchers, been quite a morning.

When everyone had caught their breath and got used to the daylight again, our heroic archaeologist rang the team in Oxford to let them know that they were safe. She was momentarily deafened by the explosion of loud cheers and happy shouting on the other end of the line.

'We're so glad that you're okay!' Edith exclaimed, after Aisha had told her all about the underground ordeal. 'The good news is that your father and Celia are now in Paris and are

close by. Stay exactly where you are and they will find you in five minutes or so.'

'What about Dimitar?' Aisha asked.

'He has been difficult to pin down,' replied Edith. 'I don't think we can rely on Mr Vakondember.'

Aisha said goodbye and hung up, disappointed. It was a blow that they did not have Dimitar and his flying machine.

As they waited for Satnam and Celia, Aisha turned to Ringo, who looked happier than he had ever looked, lying down on the grass. 'Thank you for leading Agnes to us and for pulling us to safety,' she said. 'We'd never have got out without you.'

'You're welcome,' said Ringo. 'I'm sorry I

caused you so much trouble before that,' he added, ashamed. 'I chose the wrong team. But it's hard to make friends when other people hold their noses when they look at you.'

'We all make mistakes,' said Aisha. 'I think that if you have a nice hot shower every day and try to be healthy, you might find things will improve for you.'

Agnes smiled at Ringo. 'I will take you somewhere to buy some wonderful French soap, and then you will smell delightful. And you can start by being friends with us, if you like. The street kids could do with a grown-up on their side from time to time.'

Ringo's eyes filled with fat, salty tears. It had been a long time since anyone had shown

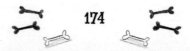

him even a sliver of good feeling. 'Thank you,' he managed to say. 'In return, I will help look after you and your friends. Maybe we can start by finding a better place for you all to live. Somewhere that is not underground.'

'Well,' began Agnes, 'I have the key that Aisha gave me. It might be worth a bit. We could see if it's enough to buy a hotel.'

'Hang on!' said Aisha, suddenly remembering something Mr Dukes had said in Oxford. 'We can have the key valued by an expert, but it doesn't matter. I just remembered that there's a reward for capturing the Grandmas. A million pounds! You should turn them in to the police.'

Agnes's eyes lit up. '*That* would buy a hotel.

A real home for me and my friends!' she said, with a clap of her hands.

Ringo was excited too. 'I can work on reception and help keep away any unwanted visitors,' he said, grinning.

Aisha smiled. *Those two will be okay,* she thought to herself as Ringo and Agnes wandered off together in search of a soap shop. 'Thank you!' she called after them. 'I will be back to see you both as soon as I can!'

The moment Ringo and Agnes disappeared around the corner, Satnam and Celia arrived in the park, both a little breathless.

Satnam hugged his daughter. 'Beta, thank goodness you are safe. I heard from Edith that you have been stuck down in the catacombs with

176

Lupton? I am so sorry we did not get here earlier. Are you both okay? What news of the treasure?'

'We're fine, Dad,' Aisha replied, 'but you need to forget about the treasure. Something far more important is going on. You'd better sit down.'

Satnam and Aisha perched on a nearby bench under a pink blossom tree, with Celia and Indiana huddled next to them. A light breeze lifted the blossom off the branches, like large pink snowflakes, which landed in Aisha's hair as she whispered urgently to her dad, 'Have you heard of the Sleeper of Ephesus?'

'Yes,' said Satnam. 'It's an old myth – about a mathematician and clockmaker who invented something rather juicy. A richly decorated golden clock of sorts.'

'Yes, Dux Temporis,' Aisha said, nodding. 'Lupton is convinced it's part of the treasure — and *that's* what he's after. He's going to use it to go back in time and make himself the richest, most powerful man on the planet. We could all wake up one morning working for Lupton.'

Satnam's face turned grey at the thought.

'What can we do?' Celia asked.

'The most useful thing we found was a stone map,' whispered Indiana. 'Aisha took some photos.'

Satnam pulled out his spectacles and examined the photos on Aisha's phone.

'Fascinating petroglyph,' he said.

'What's a petroglyph?' Celia asked.

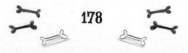

'Something carved into rock or stone,' Indiana told her.

'It's such a large area,' said Aisha, pointing out the Avenger's mark and the writing. 'It doesn't really narrow down our search.'

'There's always more to pictures like this,' said Satnam. 'Maps were the most prized possessions of a seafarer like the Avenger, and throughout history they always held their country's capital at their centre. Perhaps this map follows the same rule and has its most important part at the centre: in other words, the treasure. In which case we need to be looking here.' He pointed.

'That would be around Marseille,' said Celia.

'Aisha, email the picture to Julimus,' said Satnam. 'He's very good with this sort of thing.'

'That's what we thought too,' said Aisha. 'Done.'

Aisha loved being part of a team and felt much better about everything. 'Now I'm going to try to call Dimitar,' she said. 'He might be able to take us there in Old Meg. If not, we have another long train journey ahead of us.'

After what Edith had told her, Aisha was surprised and excited when Mr Vakondember answered immediately. She put him on speakerphone.

'Aisha! Sorry I am so late! Old Meg has been having some issues. I had to land in the

foothills of the Austrian mountains and run some repairs,' Dimitar told her. 'But don't worry. She is once more fully operational and we are now flying into Paris. Where are you?'

'Paris! We're so happy you're coming!' said Aisha. 'We need your flying machine to take us somewhere, if that's okay?'

'Landing will not be easy,' said Dimitar above the noise of engines. 'Paris is very built-up and I have no idea where to aim for.'

'Can you see the Eiffel Tower?' asked Satnam.

'Yes!' replied Dimitar. 'It is the only thing I recognise.'

'Head for it,' instructed Dr Ghatak. 'There's a long stretch of park behind the tower, with

181

plenty of space for you to land your aircraft. We'll come and find you.'

'Okay!' said Dimitar. 'See you there.'

Satnam tried to flag down a taxi but with no luck.

'Take a bike,' Celia suggested. Fortunately, there was one city bike at a terminal nearby and they grabbed it. Indiana jumped in the basket, Aisha sat on the saddle, and Satnam stood on the pedals.

'I'll contact HQ and bring the team up to speed,' said Celia as the bike pulled away. 'Good luck,' she called after them.

Pedalling furiously, our heroes headed off towards the Eiffel Tower to wait for Old Meg and Mr Dimitar Vakondember, watched by

two pigeons perched on a statue of Charles de Gaulle.

Minutes later, bike deposited, Dr Ghatak, Aisha and Bones sprinted into the Champ de Mars gardens. The Eiffel Tower stretched towards the heavens at one end, kissing the wispy French clouds that criss-crossed the deep-blue sky above the capital.

Their timing was spot on, for it wasn't long, dearest book munchers, before they became aware of something high in the sky, heading slowly but surely towards them. As they watched, shading their eyes from the sun, others too began to look towards the strange aircraft that was approaching.

Old Meg was quite a sight for the spectators, as she wibbled and wobbled towards them like a chubby old moth heading towards a lamp shop. With her circular brass-and-glass cockpit, little round porthole windows and enormous leather wings, she resembled a big friendly owl going to a fancy-dress party dressed as a bat.

The crowd roared and cheered as Dimitar brought Old Meg in to land on the lush green grass right in front of the Eiffel Tower. Aisha and her team ran to the plane as fast as they could and climbed the rope ladder that led them up into the belly of Dimitar's beautiful flying machine.

Time was of the essence. Without delay,

Aisha introduced her father to Mr Vakondember as he prepared Old Meg to take off again.

'Where to, my famous friends?' he asked over the noise of Old Meg's beefy roar.

'Marseille,' Satnam told him. 'But we're not sure where just yet.'

'*Gaah!* I KNOW WHERE!' said Indiana.

Dimitar looked very surprised at this.

'Our dog talks,' said Aisha quickly, remembering that Mr Vakondember wasn't in on the secret. 'He's magic. I'll explain later. Indiana, go on,' she urged.

'It's been on the tip of my tongue since the crypt in the Catacombs,' her scruffy pal continued. 'The writing on the map . . .

QUAERITE ANTRUM MARIS.

I remembered what it means. **SEEK THE SEA CAVE!'**

'*Seek the sea cave,*' Dimitar repeated, staring in wonder at Indiana. 'There's the Cosquer Cave just off the French coast, near Marseille. It is almost forty metres below sea level. That *does* sound like a splendid place for a knight to hide some treasure.'

'Cool,' said Aisha. 'But how on earth are we going to find treasure in a cave that is basically at the bottom of the ocean?'

'I think I might be able to help with that one too,' said Mr Vakondember, bursting with pridey excitement. 'Lucky I brought it with me.'

At the rear of Old Meg's cabin was something the size of a small car, covered in an old dust sheet. 'Take a peek at my new friend,' said Dimitar, grinning like the owner of a chutney factory.

Aisha stepped up and whipped off the cloth, revealing a little submarine. Dimitar had built it to look like a fish, with fishlike fins in the way that his plane had bat wings. It looked like Old Meg's little fishy sister.

'Wow plus wow multiplied by wow and baked in a big oven of wowzers!' Aisha gasped.

'Thanks.' Dimitar blushed. 'This is Underwater Meg. She'll deliver you right into that sea cave.'

12

Under the Sea

Back at Oxford HQ, Edith and Julimus were examining an enlarged image of the petroglyph that Aisha had sent them. They had confirmed it was a map of Europe with Marseille at its very centre, and had agreed with Indiana's translation of 'quaerite antrum maris': seek the sea cave.

'I wish we could see the carving itself,' said Edith, who was peering through an enormous magnifying glass. 'It's hard to get the sense of it from this photo.'

'The map is very similar to many I have seen in the British Museum,' said Julimus. 'If we were to enhance the image, we would perhaps see the markings of where the Lonely Avenger sailed his boat, the *Black Tiger*.'

After a moment of more careful study, he cried, 'Look! Do you see the faintest of marks here, criss-crossing the Mediterranean Sea from Egypt, Libya and Algeria, towards the south of France?'

'Just about,' said Edith from behind the magnifying glass, which made her eyeball look ten times its actual size.

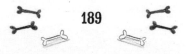

'With the right equipment, I suspect we would see a great many more lines. But I need a particular piece of software that I use at the British Museum.'

'Email the picture and jump on a fast train,' suggested Edith. 'I'll look after Jovis while you're gone.'

'Good idea. We are dancing in the dark trying to do the analysis here,' Julimus said, gathering his things. 'But it could take me a while.'

'Okay,' replied Edith. 'Call as soon as you find anything.'

'Will do,' said the shabby-suited Julimus as he headed up the stone steps.

*

Eight hundred miles away, and ten thousand feet up in the air, Aisha, Satnam and Dimitar were deep in conversation above the noise of Old Meg's chunky homemade engine, which sounded as though it was running on Hungarian goulash.

'Have you ever piloted a submarine before?' Dimitar shouted to Satnam.

'Yes,' Dr Ghatak replied. 'About twenty years ago. We were studying an underwater stone-circle at Atlit Yam, off the coast of Israel. We used a mini submarine to visit the site each day.'

'In that case, Underwater Meg should be straightforward for you,' said Dimitar. 'The controls are simple. There is a joystick, which

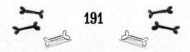

191

moves her up, down, left and right, and a throttle for speed, like a motorbike. And she has an onboard voice-activated computer,' he added with the greatest of pride. 'I only installed it yesterday, and I haven't had time to test it fully, but you can talk to her like a friend.'

'Okay,' said Satnam. 'Sounds amazing.'

They were interrupted by the sound of Dimitar's radio crackling into life.

'Hello, Dimitar – Julimus here,' said a familiar voice. 'I am on a train heading back to London to do some detailed analysis on the photo you sent. Where are you?'

Our team were excited to hear their old friend and all joined in saying a big friendly hello to him.

'We are heading to the Cosquer Cave,' Satnam told him. 'Can you provide any information about it?'

'One moment,' replied Julimus, consulting his laptop. 'Yes, I have found a map online. The entrance to the cave is underwater, but it looks as though not all the area is submerged once you get inside. You should be able to land nearby and have a look around.'

'Fantastic,' said Satnam. 'We will do that and call you as soon as we can.'

'Good luck!' replied Julimus, and hung up.

Dimitar turned to Dr Ghatak. 'I will drop Underwater Meg as close to the sea cave as I can, and then I will land on the nearest stretch of coast,' said Dimitar. 'Contact me when

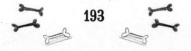

you are done, and I will come and winch you up again.'

As they approached their destination, Aisha, Indiana and Satnam clambered inside Underwater Meg and closed the door tightly. Satnam powered up the cool little submarine and established radio contact with Dimitar.

'Okay,' said Dimitar. 'Seatbelts on. Prepare to be lowered. Are you ready?'

'Yes,' replied Satnam and Aisha. Indiana Bones gulped and covered his eyes with his hairy paws.

Dimitar started counting down from ten. Aisha reached out and held her dad's hand. It's not every day that you get lowered into the sea in a tiny homemade submarine. What

if it broke down and they got chased by an angry squid or a giant spider crab? She crossed her fingers and hoped that Dimitar had made Underwater Meg as well as her airborne counterpart as the inventor finished his countdown: '... three, two, one, GO!'

The trap door in Old Meg's undercarriage opened and the smaller fishymobile was lowered carefully into the waves. When it hit the water, the rope was released, and sunshine and sky disappeared. Our heroes were submerged in a bubbly galaxy of silver froth, created by Underwater Meg plopping into the deep blue of the Mediterranean Sea.

Indiana removed his paws from his eyes and gazed in wonder at the incredible views

outside. It was like being in a brand-new world. Shards of sunlight from above sliced through the water like golden laser beams, and all around were shades of the most beautiful bright blues.

With Satnam at the controls, Underwater Meg carried them gently downwards, deeper and deeper.

Aisha thought she would check out the voice-activated computer Dimitar had mentioned.

(Note to all book munchers from Sir Harold of Heape: Anyone reading Underwater Meg's voice should do so in the style of an old-fashioned robot.)

196

'Underwater Meg, are you okay?' she asked, grinning at her dad. To her astonishment, Underwater Meg replied with the voice of an old-fashioned robot.

'*Bzzt*. Meg is operational,' came the response. 'Systems report my bottom has sent a message of wetness.'

Aisha smiled. 'Oh dear. Sorry about that.'

'No problem,' said Underwater Meg. 'These things happen when you are a submarine. *Bzzt*.'

Indiana couldn't stop staring out of the porthole. It was B.E.A.U.T.I.F.U.L. LOVELY. As they descended, shoals of colourful fish swam nearby, flicking as one and changing direction. Aisha gasped as a ray glided past,

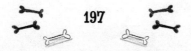

the enormous kite-shaped fish smoothly cutting through the water, as if it was flying. Peering downwards, Indiana saw that the sea floor was a mixture of golden sand and rocky outcrops. A purply green underwater forest of leaves swayed this way and that, dancing to the silent disco of the sea.

Huge areas of the rock were peppered with bright red flashes of colour.

'What are the red things, Meg?' Aisha asked.

'They are anemones,' replied Meg. 'They. Are. Very. Wiggly. *Bzzt.*'

'Look, a crab,' said Aisha, as transfixed by the scene as Indiana.

'Crabs are rubbish,' said Meg. 'They have ten eyes and their teeth are in their tummies.'

'What else do you know about crabs, Meg?' Aisha asked.

'They walk sideways and are not good at sharing.'

'What do you mean, "not good at sharing"?' Aisha asked.

'They are shellfish. Ha. Ha. Ha.'

Aisha collapsed into a fit of giggles. Dimitar had clearly given Meg a sense of humour and she was as silly as a sandpit.

Shaking his head, Indiana noticed a large lobster scuttling below them, startled by Underwater Meg's shadow on the sea floor.

Aisha saw a strange flat fish gliding just behind it. 'Meg, what's that?' she asked.

'That is a flounder,' said Meg. 'It is called a flat fish, because it is a fish and it is flat. *Bzzt.*'

They observed a big turtle trundle by on one side, and on the other was a family of seahorses, each the size of a thumb – all oblivious to our watching heroes. Aisha imagined the seahorses were on their way to an underwater sea school to do maths, PE and a whole school assembly.

Satnam, who had been concentrating hard on piloting the little sub, whispered suddenly, 'Look! Unless I am very much mistaken, we are nearing the Cosquer Cave.'

Slowly looming into view was a large dark shape, which did look as though it could be only one thing – the entrance to a cave.

'Meg, it's pretty dark up ahead,' said Satnam Ghatak. 'Do you have any headlights?'

'Yes. They are from an old Hungarian tractor,' Meg told him. 'The switch is above your head. *Bzzt*.'

Satnam flicked the switch as they approached the entrance. A beam of light from Underwater Meg cut through the darkness.

'I don't like this very much,' said Indiana Bones, who was remembering the darkness of the Catacombs.

'I know what you mean,' said Aisha, resting a reassuring hand on her pal's hairy head and

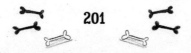

giving him a loving little ruffle. 'We'll be okay though. I promise we'll all stick together in the cave.'

Satnam Ghatak piloted Meg through the long tunnel entrance into the sea cave. Eventually the water began to get shallower and shallower, until finally Meg popped her head out of the water and the bottom of the sub bumped onto the sandy sea floor.

'We are here,' announced Meg. 'My underwater bum feels scratchy.'

Satnam trained Meg's large headlamps deep into the cave, so they illuminated the colossal space. 'Let's go,' he said.

Aisha and Satnam took out their torches and began to shine them all around. Indiana had

something much better than a strong torch – his huge, hairy hunting hooter, which was always a wonderful thing to have on a badventure.

It wasn't long before this snuffling snout picked up a familiar smell: a mixture of money and unkindness.

'I smell the Serpent,' Indiana growled quietly.

'Yuck,' said Aisha.

'Clever sausage,' said Satnam. 'Is he still here?'

'I don't think so,' Indiana said, sniffing furiously at the sand.

He stopped suddenly, and Aisha ran over and shone her torch onto the ground in front of Indiana. There were two sets of prints in the

sand. One was long, slender and pointy, and looked more as though it had been made by a pterodactyl than a human.

'The Serpent,' said Indiana, remembering the shape of the shoe to which he'd fixed the tracker. He sniffed at the second set of prints. 'Unhappy potatoes, lies and bad meat,' he said. 'These belong to Castle.'

'We were right not to trust him. He hasn't changed sides at all,' said Aisha.

Lupton, it seemed, had searched every nook of the space. Guided by their torches and Indiana's mega-conk, our heroes followed the prints towards the back of the cave. At last, Aisha spotted something glinting in the torchlight and rushed over to investigate. On

the ground they found what was left of a large torch.

Satnam shone his torch at the wall above and soon spotted an area where something had been smashed against it.

'Someone got grumpy,' said Indiana.

'Looks like he found nothing,' Satnam muttered.

'And he got so cross he smashed his torch,' said Aisha.

'Oh dear,' said Satnam. 'I feel very silly. I have just realised something.'

'What is it, Dad?' said Aisha.

'Well, this was never going to be where the treasure was hidden.'

'Why not?' Indiana Bones asked.

'Think how tricky it was for us to get in here. It would have been impossible for the Avenger to bring all his treasure down.'

'Is our knight playing more games with us, Dad?' wondered Aisha. 'Is he deliberately trying to mislead us?'

'I don't think so,' Satnam answered. 'I think we all just got carried away. We heard the translated words "Sea Cave", so we guessed and assumed Marseille without doing proper research. We blindly rushed down here, as did Lupton. I don't believe our knight has ever been here.'

Aisha and Indiana knew that Satnam was right. The mood of our intrepid archaeologists fell very flat, finding that they'd hit yet another dead end.

It was Indiana who broke the silence. 'I've had enough,' he said. 'Obsessed with treasure, chasing it all over the world, it's taken over our lives. We're as bad as Lupton.'

'We're not,' said Aisha. 'I don't care about the treasure any more, Indiana. I just want to make sure Lupton doesn't get his hands on Dux Temporis.'

'I think Lupton is as far away from finding that as any of us are from finding the treasure,' said Indiana. 'It could literally be anywhere on earth. It could be nowhere. We just don't know.'

'What would you rather do?' Satnam asked.

'I want to go to Skara Brae,' said Indiana, looking his friend in the eye. 'I want to take my

mum home and I want to say a proper goodbye to her.'

Satnam paused and looked at his beloved dog for what seemed like an eternity. 'Okay,' he said finally. 'Wise old poodle, I think you're right. Maybe it's time to start living our lives again.'

13

A Medium-Sized Chapter Where Something Very Bad Happens

One single, solitary day later, almost the whole of our team was once again gathered

at Charman and Dukes in the centre of Oxford. Indiana Bones was present, of course. And Aisha was there with Satnam, Celia, Edith, Mr Charman, Mr Dukes, Jovis and Dimitar Vakondember. Julimus, you remember, had gone to London to examine the photo of the petroglyph with special equipment at the British Museum.

I am sorry to say that Aisha was still feeling flatter than a roti, flatter than a frisbee, and flatter than the flounder she'd glimpsed in the Mediterranean, just the day before.

'We have done our best, my darlings!' said Edith, forcing a light-hearted laugh and trying to lift the mood.

'Adventures can be like this,' said Dr Ghatak to his daughter. 'Sometimes we just need to regroup. Now we must do this important thing for Indiana. Let's take him to Skara Brae. You and I can talk long and hard about the Lonely Avenger. When we get home, we can plan our next move. We will have to wait and see.'

Wait and see, Aisha thought to herself. This was a phrase that she had never liked. In her experience, it was always just another way for a groan-up to say *NO*. She felt like crying. However, she recognised that they needed to do an important thing for Indiana, and so she put on her bravest face and gave the smallest of nods to her dad.

*

Meanwhile, upstairs, something very sneaky and naughty was going on. Philip Castle had returned to Charman and Dukes and was now standing outside. Several days ago, he had taken the Blu-Tack with the imprint of the shop key to a dark corner of Oxford. Down a wiggly alley was a locksmith who had once been a burglar and safe-cracker. Castle had paid him to make a copy of the key. Thinking the shop was empty, Castle was turning his naughty key in the lock in the travel agents' door. After the disappointment of the Cosquer Cave, our baddies too had reached a dead end in their search for the treasure. Castle hoped that a bit of eavesdropping at Charman and Dukes might help them get back on the trail. Quietly

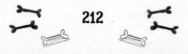

he slipped in, silent as a sausage in a sock, and began to sneak around.

At the back of the shop, Castle the worm was delighted to find the false bookcase open. Oh dear, lovely book munchers, with the shop door locked, our team had become rather complacent about closing the bookcase.

'Will you take a looky here,' Castle said to himself, grinning.

He leaned inside, thrilled to hear voices below, and craned his neck to listen to what the Good Team were up to. He hoped to trade this intelligence with the Serpent to get properly back in his good books. After the mysterious disappearance of the Grandmas, Lupton had given Castle another chance. Castle

was determined not to muck things up and was optimistic that he might even be able to negotiate a bigger portion of the treasure — if he could get them back on the right track. He'd been waiting all his life for a slice of the treasure pie. He believed it was his birthright, as he was a direct descendent of Diane, the Lonely Avenger's true love. Our knight had stolen many treasures to build a shrine for Diane. To Castle, it seemed only right that he should have his share of these riches.

'So, we are all in agreement then? Raise your hands,' he heard Edith say. 'Good. Everybody.'

At the top of the stone staircase, Castle grinned to himself at his own cleverness

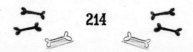

and pulled out a little notebook and pencil in case he needed to record something gigantically juicy.

'I'm convinced this is the right thing,' said Dr Ghatak. 'We need to get up to Scotland – to the Orkneys and Skara Brae. Aisha and I will go with Indiana.'

'Bingo,' said Castle to himself, scribbling it all down.

'I will make your travel arrangements,' said Mr Dukes. 'Train and taxi should do it. Then perhaps a local fisherperson to get you to Skara Brae itself.'

'Gotcha, Ghataks,' said Castle. Then, realising that Mr Dukes was slowly heading upstairs and was about to catch him spying,

Castle pocketed his notebook and slipped back out of the front door, making sure to lock it behind him.

At a safe distance from the shop, Castle disappeared into an alleyway and pulled out his phone to call Lupton.

The Serpent answered immediately. 'This had better be good,' he said, not even bothering to say hello.

'I have new information,' replied Castle, feeling as clever as a cat on a cushion. 'The Ghataks are on the move. We were a million miles away, sir. If we can settle on the idea of me having a very modest fifteen per cent of whatever we find, I will lead us both straight to the treasure.'

The slithery Serpent turned super-silent, pondering over what he was hearing.

'Deal,' he said finally. 'Where is the treasure?'

'It's in Scotland,' said Castle. 'They are going to take a train up there imminently.'

'Do the Ghataks know that you know?' enquired Lupton.

'They don't have a clue.'

'Good,' replied the Serpent. 'You have done well, Castle, and you shall have your share. Come to the office and tell me everything. We'll take the helicopter up to Scotland and be there long before their pathetic train. And we'll take an enormous leash, the kind that professional dog catchers use. It is time that

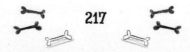

we took control of the meddling mutt. Perhaps the ghastly Ghataks will trade the treasure for their dumb dog.'

What a mess with a pickle on top! Castle was, of course, a monumental bum-hat who'd picked up totally the wrong end of the stick. The journey to Skara Brae was for Indiana, not lost treasure. Either way, it was bad news for our team. And worse, it was not going to be the quiet goodbye that Indiana had been longing for.

14

Indiana Bones
Goes Home

The journey to Scotland was wonderfully
restful. A sense of calm had wrapped itself
around Indiana like an extremely snug and
friendly blanket. It was so nice to feel like they

were not being chased, and to feel as though they were not chasing anything either. For the first time since five past forever, our heroes had been able to zonk out and relax. Lupton was a dim and distant memory and that, to Mr Indiana Bones, felt nine times as nice as a horse in a hat.

The elderly gentlemen of travel, Mr Charman and Mr Dukes, had used their excellent knowledge to book Indiana and his friends on a wonderful old steam locomotive called *Sunrise*. They had their own cabin with seats, bunks and a window so they could watch the world glide by. The steam train was nearly two hundred years old, and once a month it chugged slowly from

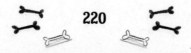

London to Scotland, with the first stop on the journey conveniently being Oxford. Our friends played board games, gobbled up book after delicious book, and feasted on a great many tasty snacks. Being on board this lazy train made it easy to forget about the Avenger's treasure.

Sunrise took them as far as Inverness and from there they hired a car, which Dr Ghatak drove all the way up to Thurso on the northernmost tip of Scotland. There they met an old friend of Mr Charman and Mr Dukes, known as Salty Susan. She had been fishing the waters around Orkney for more than fifty years, and clearly there was no better person to take them from the mainland to Indiana's

family home of Skara Brae on the main Orkney island.

Indiana stood at the bow of the boat, nose in the air sniffing, while Aisha and Satnam sat in the cabin and listened to Salty Susan telling tall tales about fish she'd caught and storms she'd wrestled in *Cleopatra*, her cute little fishing boat. A seagull with a big yellow beak and mean beady eyes sat on top of the cabin; he'd been with them since they left the mainland. Salty Susan said the bird often travelled with her because he was too lazy to fly. She called him Naughty Peter.

'There was much excitement yesterday,' Susan said to Satnam. 'A big helicopter landed on the island.'

'Oh, really,' said Satnam. 'I wonder what for.'

'Oil company, probably,' said Susan. 'They're always sticking their beaks in here where they're not wanted.'

At *Cleopatra*'s bow, Indiana continued to sniff at the wet, salty air, thinking his own private thoughts. He hadn't been back here since he was a puppy and realised for the first time that it made him Scottish, which he rather liked. He thought about his mum. Meeting Amie was, to Indiana, worth more than all the treasure in the world. Our hairy hero wished he'd been able to spend more time with her. He had a hundred and one questions about his home and his family, and not for the first time he wondered about his dad.

Aisha emerged from the cabin and wrapped an arm around him, pulling him in for a cuddle. As they sat quietly together, a pair of seals and their pup popped out of the water just in front of them.

'Hey, Indiana, why do seals live in salt water?' Aisha said, rubbing the underside of her best pal's belly.

'I don't know,' replied Indiana, very much enjoying the tummy rub.

'Because pepper makes them sneeze!' said Aisha.

Indiana turned to look at his friend. 'You should stick to archaeology,' he said. 'I've had funnier trips to the doggy dentist.'

'Harsh but fair,' Aisha giggled. 'Ooh, look! Land ahoy!'

Sure enough, the Orkney Islands were coming into view.

Aisha grinned. 'I've always wanted to say that. Makes me feel like a pirate.'

As *Cleopatra* neared land, the skies became busy with more seagulls and Aisha spotted puffins too, which were surprisingly small and ever so adorable.

Satnam came out to join them. 'Susan is taking us to the west coast of the main island, to the Bay of Skaill. That's where we'll land. It's just a short walk from there to Skara Brae.'

'That's where you were born, Indiana,' said Aisha, cuddling her pal once more.

'I know,' said Indiana, suddenly nervous. The sapphire in his collar began to glow.

Seven hundred and fifteen miles away in London, Julimus was in his office at the British Museum, looking at an enlarged image of the stone map on his computer. The details had been super-enhanced by specialist software. He'd been studying the map for the last few days, but the puzzle wasn't getting much clearer. The criss-crossing of lines in the Mediterranean went everywhere and nowhere – and, to Julimus's tired eyes, they now looked like a dropped packet of spaghetti.

Our gentle friend knew that several thousand years ago the Mediterranean Sea was

one of the major trade routes of the world. The merchants who'd travelled these routes had been Roman, Persian and Greek. It followed that the Lonely Avenger may have used the maps of these traders, or followed their boats, or even had crew members who had sailed the routes before. Evidence of this was in front of Julimus now. There seemed to be a million of these journeys all over the map.

This was all very fascinating, but it only confirmed to Julimus what they already knew: that the Lonely Avenger had spent his time zig-zagging the sea, presumably looting and stealing and filling the *Black Tiger* with swag to build a shrine to his beloved.

Our shabby-suited friend had been working

long hours in his office, deep in the belly of the British Museum. He was often still there late at night when the cleaner came in. Today she was much earlier than usual.

'Hello, Julimus,' said her familiar voice, as she reached for the wastepaper basket under his desk.

'Oh, hello, Jane,' said Julimus. He leaned back in his chair and smiled, propping his glasses on his forehead and rubbing his tired eyes.

'Here all night again? Haven't you got a home to go to?' asked the ever-friendly cleaner.

'I do have a home to go to, Jane, but this map won't let me,' sighed Julimus. 'It has tied me up in knots. I am its prisoner.'

'What's the problem?' Jane asked, looking over his shoulder.

'Well,' began Julimus, 'the lines you can see are trade routes in the Mediterranean. Believe it or not, I am hoping that they will lead me to something fascinating.'

'Ooh. Something fascinating? Now that would keep a man up all night,' chuckled Jane.

'Indeed,' said Julimus. 'But I'm completely stuck, to be honest.'

'Let me have a look,' said Jane.

Julimus smiled. 'Why not?' he said. With a pencil, he began pointing at the various lines. 'These are the journeys of a boat with an *interesting cargo*. We've searched in Egypt; we've searched in Turkey, and in France too.

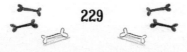

But it's impossible to tell where to look next — how do we know which line to follow?'

Jane studied the map. 'How about that one all on its own?' she asked.

'There is no line on its own,' said Julimus.

'Here,' said Jane, pointing. 'It goes out of the Med and up the side of Ireland, all the way to those little islands at the top.'

'Sadly, I think that's just the edge of the map, Jane,' said Julimus.

'Looks like a line to me,' said Jane. 'Like the criss-cross ones, only loads fainter. It sneaks along the top of Scotland to those islands. I bet that's where your *interesting cargo* went.'

Julimus hurriedly put his glasses back on and peered very closely at the image.

'Holy moly and jam roly-poly!' he exclaimed, standing up. He pulled Jane into an embrace, which knocked his glasses all askew, then did a little jig around the office. 'Jane, you are a genius! Perhaps even a Janius! Bless your excellent eyes. How embarrassing for me! You have found in a moment what I have spent days searching for.'

'My pleasure,' said Jane. 'I do it all the time. My husband's rubbish at looking for stuff too.'

Julimus examined the map again, this time with a magnifying glass. The newly found line did indeed go all the way up the very edge of the map before looping over to the Orkney Isles.

'Jane – thank you, thank you, thank you!

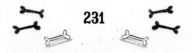

231

And now I must go and make a phone call,' he
said. And with that our shabby-suited friend
darted out of the door.

15

Shark in the Shadows

Aisha admired the way Salty Susan brought *Cleopatra* right into the southernmost corner of the Bay of Skaill. The experienced fisherwoman skilfully negotiated the cove's rocky outcrops at the points where land met sea, and soon they were gliding into the shallow waters close to the beach and preparing to plop anchor.

After being cooped up on a steam train, in a stuffy car and finally on Salty Susan's boat, Indiana was as restless as a rooster at the break of day. 'Mind if I run ahead?' he asked, as soon as they were on land.

'No, you go,' said Satnam. 'We'll meet you at Skara Brae.'

Aisha, clutching the jar containing the ashes of Amie and the Lonely Avenger, agreed. 'Run, fruit flake, run. You'll feel better for a wander around your old home afterwards.'

Indiana didn't need telling twice.

He disappeared into the distance like a hairy cannonball.

As they walked, Satnam said to Aisha, 'So, how are you feeling about all this?'

'Nervous for Indiana,' admitted Aisha. 'I just hope he's okay. He's been so keen to bring his mum back here. It's been on his mind since we got back from Turkey.'

'I wondered if he might want to return one day,' Satnam said, looking around. 'After all, this is where it all began. This is where I found him as a sleeping pup.'

Aisha smiled up at her dad. 'I know. I love that story.'

'I felt so bad that I had taken him from his home,' continued Satnam, 'but an ancient and

strong magic was at work and I had no way to return him.'

'But you brought him home and we loved him so much,' said Aisha. 'I do think he has been very happy with us.'

'I do too,' agreed Satnam. 'I think this really is for his mum. To let her rest somewhere familiar, and to say goodbye.'

'And it's goodbye to the Avenger too,' said Aisha. 'And maybe his treasure. I guess it's just too well hidden to be found by a little girl and her dog.'

'You came mighty close.' Satnam smiled, and he took his daughter's hand as they neared the ancient site of Skara Brae.

Aisha's spine tingled as she cast her

eyes over the ancient village. Older than Stonehenge and the pyramids, Skara Brae was an archaeologist's dream. She'd seen photos of course, and read about it in books, but that was nothing in comparison to being right there in the flesh, with the salty wind whipping around them.

It wasn't long before they were joined by Indiana Bones.

'How're you doing, ladoo?' Aisha asked, kneeling on the grass to rub her friend's ears and give him a snout kiss.

'It's good to be here,' said Indiana. 'I've been having a bit of a think and I want to say thank you. I love being your dog and living in your home and all the things we do. I would never

wish for anything different. I just need to do the right thing for my first family. For my mum.'

'Hey, we were saying pretty much exactly that about five seconds ago!' said Aisha.

'And our home will always be your home,' Satnam reassured him.

'We want to be here with you,' Aisha added. 'What's good for you is good for us.'

'That's how our family works,' said Satnam.

As they stroked and cuddled Indiana, a strong wind was gathering around Skara Brae. It blew Indiana's ears about till they resembled the whirring blades of a hairy helicopter.

Aisha laughed. 'We should call you Windiana! Now, don't you take off and land in Iceland!'

'Say hello to Orkney's famous land breeze,' said Satnam. 'I remember it well; it blows offshore from land to water.'

'It's a bit more than a breeze,' said Indiana, who was now looking like a whirr and blur of fur.

'Careful it doesn't blow your hair into the sea, Dad,' said Aisha.

Satnam stood up, ignoring his daughter's cheeky comment.

'See over there, Indiana,' he said, pointing to a walled, rectangular hole in the ground. 'That's the exact spot where I found you. When I was here last, it was a muddy pit, but now it's been properly excavated and restored. See how well preserved it is, with a connecting

passage to the other houses in the village, and they've built the passageway roofs too. All that was totally hidden before.'

Indiana padded over. 'It feels special,' he said. 'It's exactly the right place to scatter the ashes.'

'Yes, it is,' agreed Aisha.

'When would you like to do that?' Satnam asked.

'I don't know,' replied Indiana, suddenly wobbly. 'I'm not sure that I'm quite ready yet. I'm sorry.'

'Hey, no worries,' said Satnam. 'Take all the time you need.'

Now, dearest book munchers, while this was all rather nice and wholesome, things were

about to get fruity. Just a few metres away, hiding in one of the connecting passages, were none other than the Serpent Lupton and his double-crossing sidekick, Philip Castle. They'd arrived by helicopter the day before. They'd seen our heroes land on the beach, and they'd followed them to Skara Brae. Now they were eavesdropping on the Ghataks and waiting to pounce.

Standing at the edge of the excavation, Indiana snuffled at the air. With his mega-conk, our hero might normally have been able to pick up the scent of his foes, but the wind was in the wrong direction – and yet there was something distracting him. He was about to speak when Satnam's phone began to ring.

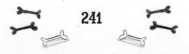

'Hello, Julimus, old friend,' said Dr Ghatak.

'Hello, Satnam. You're in a group call. I have news! I'm in London and the others are joining from Oxford.'

'Hello!' shouted the rest of the Good Team from their base below Charman and Dukes.

'Aisha and Indiana are here too,' said Satnam. 'What news, Julimus?'

'Huge news!' replied his friend. 'News so big I can barely keep still. I think that the lost treasure is hidden near Skara Brae. Is there a sea cave on the main island?'

Satnam thought for a second. 'There *is* a collapsed sea cave, if I remember correctly. It's called the Gloup.'

Lupton, lurking like a shark in the shadows,

gripped Castle's arm so hard it nearly made his sidekick cry out.

'You must head there immediately,' said Julimus. 'I think that is where you'll find the *Black Tiger*!'

Satnam glanced at Aisha, and then at Indiana, who was looking downcast again.

'We're not hunting treasure today,' said Aisha, resting a hand on Indiana's head. 'No way. Nor tomorrow. Nor even the next day.'

'Sorry, Julimus. It will have to wait,' said Satnam. 'Some things are more important than treasure, and Indiana is one of those things.'

Julimus understood completely. 'Yes, of course. It has stayed hidden for two thousand years; a little longer won't hurt,' he said.

'Indiana, we all send our love. Your mother would be very proud of you.'

'Hear, hear!' echoed the whole team. 'Love you, Indiana!'

Indiana lifted his head, smiled and let out three loud barks, meaning, *Thank you, thank you, thank you.*

Lupton couldn't believe his ears. 'Imbeciles,' he whispered, sounding angrier than a boiling kettle.

When Satnam had ended the call, Indiana Bones looked up and nodded gently, to show that he was ready.

Our three friends climbed down into the large chamber where Satnam had found Indiana. 'Aisha, would you scatter the ashes for

244

me?' Indiana asked.

She took the top off the jar and started to sprinkle the remains of the Avenger and Amie around the chamber, while Indiana spoke in a gentle whisper:

'Thank you, Mum, and thank you, Lonely Avenger. I am so glad we managed to meet each other. I wish I could see you one last time, but I'm happy that we've been able to bring you home to Skara Brae so you can rest in peace with your people.'

Indiana's sapphire began to glow, and for some reason he felt the urge to quietly chant the exact same words that Satnam had chanted in this very chamber when he'd found Indiana as a pup.

Om Sah Maatraa Namah

Om Sah Maatraa Namah

Om Sah Maatraa Namah

Aisha and Satnam joined in, murmuring,

Om Sah Maatraa Namah

As they chanted, something thincredible and funbelievable happened. Just like when Satnam had been here last, an age-old charm was triggered. Ancient magic crackled loudly through the chamber and they became enveloped in a silver mist. Bright white sparkles fizzed, while flickers of light zipped and danced around them. A dense electric fog filled the ancient space until it was impossible for them to see even as far as the end of their noses. There came an enormous crack of thunder and a brilliant white flash of lightning, then the air cleared and they could see once more.

They now stood in a sumptuous room with red walls, and a big copper door had appeared in the wall opposite. Slowly the door opened and out stepped the Lonely Avenger, with Amie by his side. Behind them were three robed figures, the clan chiefs who protected Skara Brae.

'Welcome,' said the knight with a smile. 'How lovely to see you again.'

'Hello,' said Aisha, thrilled to see her knight.

'Thank you for bringing me home,' said Amie to Indiana.

The knight smiled. *'To the best place in the world.'*

Aisha, her dad and Indiana all looked at each other, utterly speechless.

'You wished to see me one last time, so come inside,' said Amie. 'Meet your father, and your brothers and sisters too. All of you, come.'

The Avenger and Amie turned and headed back through the large copper door with the three kings. Indiana, Aisha and her dad followed, amazed and at a loss for words.

Unfortunately, dear readers, they were not alone. Just before the ancient magic dissipated and closed the secret entrance, a snake and

248

a rat – Lupton and Castle – scurried like cockroaches across the chamber and slipped in through the copper door after them.

16
Skara Talamh

When our friends stepped through the door, they found themselves pushing their way through thick low-hanging branches, bushes and undergrowth.

'I don't understand,' said Aisha. 'Plants can't grow underground. What's going on?'

'No idea,' her dad replied, struggling through the thicket. 'But there's magic in the air. Just follow the clan chiefs.'

Satnam, Aisha and Indiana followed with some difficulty for a few minutes until finally they stepped out of the thick vegetation and onto a small hillside, which sloped gently down towards the shore of a large underground lake. What they could see beyond the lake was the most fantastic sight. Spread out below, on the other side of the water, was a beautiful walled city. At its centre was a huge dark castle, medieval in style, with towers and pointed roofs, and it shimmered a little, as if it was slightly out of focus. Gazing at the magical subterranean metropolis,

they almost felt as though they had been transported into an enormous fairy-tale land. There were towers and lights and houses and bridges. A twinkly river fed the lake, the far edge of which was dotted with beaches and fir trees, where there were shadowy figures and small fishing boats.

'Welcome to Skara Talamh,' said one of the clan chiefs, who, they now noticed, floated spectre-like in front of them.

'Wow!' said Aisha. 'I don't know what I was expecting, but it wasn't this. This is a whole city hidden underground . . . an invisible city.'

'It's wonderful,' Satnam agreed, taking in the beauty before him.

'It is our home,' said the king.

Just below them, towards the bottom of the hill, was a sight even more magical to our friend Indiana Bones. There was a campfire, and around it a gang of dogs was resting, snuggling and enjoying the warmth of the orange flames.

Amie trotted over to join them and summoned Indiana to come too. Aisha and her dad held hands and watched from a distance as Indiana nuzzled and snuffled with his brothers and his sisters. They were soon joined by a larger dog, who they guessed was Indiana's father.

'This looks like the best place in the world for our Indiana right now,' said Satnam.

I hid the treasure in the best place in the

world. Aisha remembered the knight's riddle and looked around. 'It is,' she said.

At those words, the sapphire in our hero's necklace began to glow like a beacon.

'Look at that!' said Satnam, noticing the glow coming from his own sapphire. 'Do you suppose Indiana's love for his family is causing the reaction?'

'Or something else,' Aisha replied, suddenly feeling a little uneasy. She scanned the area around them for possible causes.

Over in the doggy-snuggle, Amie spoke to her son. 'Thank you for bringing me back to my family. Now we can rest and be happy.'

'The knight has told me about the kind of dog that you have become,' said Indiana's

father. 'We are proud of you, and your new family.' The older dog lifted his chin to show that he too had a sapphire in his collar, as did all the brothers and sisters. 'Remember, we are all linked by a deep magic and we will always be in each other's lives, connected by our dreams.'

'Thank you,' said Indiana. This was wonderfully reassuring to our scruffy hero and he felt happier than he'd been for a long time.

The Lonely Avenger approached Satnam and Aisha. 'I am glad that you are getting closer to my treasure. I have always wanted you to find it. I know you will use my fortune wisely.'

'We've stopped looking for the treasure,' said Aisha. 'We're here for Indiana.'

'You don't want it?' asked the knight.

'Not really,' Aisha replied. 'We never wanted the treasure for ourselves anyway. We wanted to return it to where it belongs and use the money to build schools, hospitals and libraries. Treasure on its own is kind of pointless.'

At these words, the air below them above the edge of the lake began to wobble like jelly. Magic was in the air, dear readers, and it was getting restless.

The knight's face lit up. 'Enchantment number one is broken.'

'Excuse me?' Satnam asked, confuzzled.

'I placed some rather clever enchantments on my treasure,' the knight told him. 'The first

ensured that the only people who could find the treasure were those who don't want it. The enchantment removes greedy snakes from the equation. Rather clever, don't you think?'

The view below them looked sharper, somehow. Gone was the sense that everything was out of focus. The water was crystal clear, and the air around them felt soft and fresh. Aisha and Satnam now saw that a little forest of pine trees and a beach had appeared along the near side of the lake. On a tiny island in the middle of the lake was a single, solitary tree, bathed in a shaft of light from somewhere above.

Quaerite antrum maris. Seek the sea cave. All of a sudden, they realised they were in the

sea cave they had been searching for, and it felt as though the air was buzzing with magic.

'I'm almost certain the entrance to this world is through the Gloup,' whispered Satnam to Aisha. 'A ship could have sailed directly into here hundreds of years ago – and that's what the knight must have done. Over time, the entrance to the cave collapsed, and the boat was sealed off and hidden from the rest of the world. It's the perfect hiding place for the Lost Treasure.'

Yet, no matter how hard they looked, there was no sign of the Avenger's ship – no *Black Tiger* laden with treasure.

'I'm beginning to think that your treasure doesn't exist,' said Satnam. 'Is it a trick? Have

you played us all like a banjo, or are you trying to teach us something?'

The knight just smiled and said, 'I love enchantments. They are so *enchanting.*'

On the hillside, the dogs were unaware of all this, or if they were aware, they didn't care. Indiana was having the time of his life, rolling around with his siblings and talking to his mum and his dad. This was heaven to him and he was making sure that he treasured every single minute. In fact, he was so happy that he was oblivious to the fact that his collar was flashing like a lighthouse. Danger, dear readers, was slowly edging towards our hairy hero.

Watching our team from the safety of

the thicket above them was the beast of our book, Sir Henry Lupton. He had witnessed the enchanted air change above the lake, and his snakey little mouth was watering at the prospect of what might be about to appear.

'Time to spoil the party,' he said, smiling cruelly as he shoved Castle forward to do his dirty work.

Carefully, Castle snuck down the small hillside towards the dogs. When he was close enough, he threw a leash, like a lasso, through the air. It caught Indiana around the neck and he was dragged away from his family. Indiana's father barked loudly.

Aisha turned at the sound, and her world came crashing down as she watched Castle

260

hauling her beloved pal to where the slippery Serpent was waiting.

She screamed: '*Noooooooo!!!*'

Lupton was thrilled with himself. 'Well, well, well, ghastly Ghataks,' he gloated. 'We meet again and, what fun, I seem to have the upper hand as usual. So now that I have your dumb dog on the end of a rope, are you going to give me what I want or shall I just make sure you never see him again?'

'You give him back or I will come for you!' Aisha yelled.

'Oh no. A little girl. I'm so scared,' sneered Lupton.

'What you want is not there,' Satnam shouted. 'We've all been on a wild goose chase.'

'As always, you will have missed something critical,' Lupton said scornfully. 'I suppose I shall have to come and work it out for myself,' he hissed, before making his way towards them.

When he reached the lower part of the hill, he could see that there was indeed no huge boat, no treasure and therefore no Dux Temporis. Fuming with rage, the vile Serpent picked up a rock and hurled it across the water with a curse.

Aisha watched the flight of Lupton's rock as it sailed through the air and she noticed something strange happen. The rock stopped in mid-air, as if it had struck something, and then dropped straight down. There it

bounced on something else before it gradually disappeared – as if swallowed by an invisible jelly. Something was happening below that none of them could see properly.

'*Invisibilia videre*,' Aisha whispered the words on her shield to herself.

When she had tried to use the shield in this mode in the Catacombs, nothing had happened. But now she understood. Of course! It would only work if there was actually something invisible to see, so she could *see the unseen*!

Aisha pulled the shield off her back. Placing her thumb over the sapphire, she inhaled deeply and looked up. The shield cast a blue laser-like beam up into the air. She pointed the beam towards the point where Lupton had

thrown the rock. The blue light hit what looked like an invisible glass dome. It turned that dome a lighter blue colour and revealed a sight so marvellous and funbelievable that she sank to her knees.

Enchantment number two, she heard the knight's voice whisper in her head.

The now-transparent blue dome melted to nothing and there, bobbing in the water, was the *Black Tiger* — the King of Spain's best warship, stolen two thousand years ago by the Lonely Avenger. Her sails rippled gently in the breeze. She was nothing short of majestic and her deck was overflowing with treasure.

Aisha turned to Lupton and shouted, 'Give

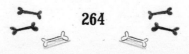

us back Indiana and you can have it all. We don't want it!'

Lupton, however, wanted whatever was aboard the *Black Tiger* more than anything else, certainly more than he wanted Mr Indiana Bones.

'I need your word that this is not another trick, Ghatak,' said Lupton, glaring at Aisha.

'I swear on my dog's life,' she replied.

This seemed to be all the promise that Lupton needed. He clicked his fingers at Castle, who released Indiana. Aisha's number-one love raced back to her side.

Lupton barked at Castle to help him aboard the ship.

Castle bellowed back. 'This treasure is owed to my family. We are Spanish royalty and this

fortune is our birthright. I want your word that I will have my share.'

'Oh, don't worry, Mr Castle,' said the Serpent. 'I promise you will get what's coming to you.'

The terrible pair raced down to the water and waded out to the *Black Tiger*. Our team watched as the Serpent trampled all over Castle to get a foothold as he began to climb a rope ladder on the outside of the ship, leaving Castle floundering in the water. When his sidekick finally did manage to climb the hull, Lupton was there at the top, waiting to stamp on his fingers.

'No one tells me what to do, you filthy worm!' roared Lupton. 'When I find Dux

Temporis, you'll get what's coming to you, all right – down in the gutter with the Ghataks!'

And with one vicious stamp on Castle's fingers, the Serpent sent him back overboard into the cold, dark lake once more.

Everybody watched in horror as Lupton raced around the deck, laughing. Then he paused, as though something monumental was about to happen. It was. He heard a sound that he'd dreamed of a great many times.

Tick-tick-tick-tick-tick-tick-tick-tick . . .

It was Dux Temporis! Lupton laughed nastily and began scurrying around the deck, peering and listening at the mounds of treasure. At last, he stopped, knee-deep in necklaces and gold and silver. Bending down,

269

he began to dig through the treasure — and there it was, Dux Temporis, hidden within a ruby-encrusted crown. Lupton took it in his hands and rushed to the side of the ship, holding it aloft for all to see.

'I have it, you filthy swines! I have it! Dux Temporis. Now the world will be mine and it shall serve me and my family for all eternity.'

Aisha was in tears as the full horror of Lupton's victory dawned on her. She turned to the knight and sobbed, 'What have I done?'

The Lonely Avenger simply smiled. 'Enchantment three,' he said, offering Aisha his open hand. 'Let the living and the dead hold hands.'

Aisha took his hand and her father's too.

They were joined by the three clan chiefs and formed a circle. The dogs formed another circle, nose to tail, around the humans. Instinctively, they all slowly walked together, round and round.

The air began to crackle, and jagged, angry sparks flew past in gusts. Around them the air felt as though it was fizzing as pressure grew. It was like being in the eye of the world's angriest storm.

During this stormy turmoil of electrically charged greed, Castle managed to climb back on board the *Black Tiger*. He rushed at Lupton and tried to wrestle Dux Temporis from his boss. The two villains were boiling like angry kettles, bubbling over with righteous belief

that they alone should triumph. Aisha hated to see anyone fighting and hid under her dad's arm, peeping at her enemies as they tumbled and fought and yelled in fury.

Just as Aisha felt as though she could bear it no more, a bolt of pure white light forked down from above, blasting both baddies. A surge of white heat melted Dux Temporis, turning it to molten liquid as Lupton watched. Castle and the Serpent were pulled up into the air while they struggled and screamed angrily, but there was no way for them to free themselves from this supernatural grip and they were pulled higher and higher. At last there was an almighty thunderclap and they were whipped up through a hole in the ceiling

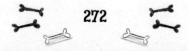

and swallowed by the sky itself.

Without warning, the ground of Skara Talamh began to shake.

'Magical aftershock,' warned the knight. 'This area is not safe.'

Everyone watched in wonder as the cave wall split and a chasm next to the lake opened up, forming a passageway to the sea.

'What are you waiting for?' said the knight. 'Get yourselves aboard.'

Aisha, Indiana and her dad rushed down towards the beach and the ship, which began to float towards them. They waded into the lake and strode purposefully through the water. Helping each other as best they could, they reached the old ship and climbed up the

dangling rope ladder. At last, they all managed to make it to the deck and collapsed in a soggy, happy heap.

As the *Black Tiger* sailed away with them, they stood and waved goodbye, knowing that this really was the last time anyone would see the clan chiefs, Indiana's family and the Lonely Avenger himself, who waved and shouted, 'Be safe, my friends, and spend my fortune well.'

'We will!' shouted Aisha.

They kept waving and waving and waving as the ship left the Gloup. The magical chasm closed behind them, sealing in the invisible city of Skara Talamh once more, and our triumphant team headed out into the open sea.

Exhausted, our heroes sank down onto the

deck, feeling properly safe for the first time in forever. Indiana lay across Aisha and Satnam, wagging his tail. He felt so lucky to have two families. That was all the treasure he would ever need.

Aisha sat and looked at the mountain of gold and jewels and precious artefacts that spilled out of the ship's hold. 'Look how much of it there is!'

It was indeed the greatest haul of treasure known to man, woman or police sniffer dog. There were trillions of pounds' worth of gold bars, jewellery, silver ingots, crowns, sceptres, mitres, rubies, sapphires, diamonds and so very much more. If I were to list it all in detail, it would need its own chapter. Alas, I must

inform you, dearest wonderful book munchers, that the book you hold in your hands has now officially run out of chapters. All that remains for me to tell you is that Aisha looked at Indiana and her dad and they looked back at her.

'We did it,' she said to them. 'We did it. We did it. We did it. I can't believe we actually did it!'

THE END

Epilogue

So that, my lovely book pals, was that. All that you need to know rests in this very last slender section of slimportant funformation. The knight had kept careful records of where he had looted, which Aisha and Indiana found in the captain's cabin of the *Black Tiger*. Indiana and Satnam and Aisha kept their word about

what they would do with it. They returned as much as possible to where it came from, and started to do good things with everything that was left.

New schools and libraries began to pop up all over the world, each with a little picture somewhere inside of the Lonely Avenger and his faithful friend, Amie. Our kind knight had started out wanting to build a shrine to a lost love but ended up with a legacy far more widespread, wonderful and worthwhile.

The *Black Tiger* herself was turned into an enormous library and was filled with the best children's books ever written. She travelled up and down the Thames, around the British Isles, and even all around the world.

Children from every continent visited and borrowed books.

You will be glad to hear that Agnes Swagness and Ringo did indeed set up a hotel in Paris for children who had, for whatever reason, lost their homes. The first time Aisha and Indiana visited, they saw that Ringo was very much a changed man. For the first time in many years, he was happy. He wore a sharp suit and sat at the reception desk of L'Hôtel Pour les Enfants Perdus. Gone were his trademark rings, and gone was the pong. He smelled, delightfully, of *Rose et Géranium*, his favourite French soap.

Julimus and Satnam continued working as archaeologists, writing book after book

and giving talks in every continent. Jovis too would often travel with Julimus and was fast becoming an expert on Egyptology and the pyramids. Celia went back to being a boring loss adjuster (*shh, dearest book munchers, let's not say any more about her being a cat burglar, just in case any police dogs are being read this as their bedtime story*).

Aisha got a Saturday job working in the cafe at a museum of art and archaeology in Oxford. She would sneak Indiana Bones in each time she worked, hiding him under her invisibility shield, and feed him little pieces of smoked salmon and tuna when no one was looking.

During her breaks, she and Indiana would

walk through the museum and look at all the wonderful artefacts on display and make up exciting stories about where each item had come from and how they had been found.

Indiana and Aisha had a whole Harry Heape of fun, playing in the museum and having discussions about treasure troves, hidden islands and marvellous sandwiches, until one day, quite out of the blue, adventure called on them once more.

And that, dearest chapter-munching book friends, is it. Thanks for sharing this glistening gladventure with me. You have been wonderful company. It's been hella fun for me to tell the tale, and I hope it has been as much fun for you to read.

Now that you've finished this book, go and get another one – there're loads of them. Visit a library. Our knight would like that. If he could tell you one thing, as you close the last page of his story, it would be this: keep reading, keep reading, keep reading, for books are the real treasure and have magic in their pages.

Your friend,
Sir Harold of Heape